VALLEY FEVER

by Wendy Padilla

To those who've lived some of Valley Fever's terror and others who have helped me understand it, and still others who have helped me write about it:

Julio Martinez
Alice Ekberg
Bill Largo
John Kehrli
Jane Harding
The Arizona Sonora Desert Museum
Brian Brockmeier
Larry Houghton
Craig Chandler, DVM
Donovon Ricketts, DO
and Donna Simko

Thank you!
Wendy Padilla

This novel is a work of fiction. Any references to real events and locales are intended only to give the fiction a sense of reality and authenticity. Any resemblance to actual persons, living or dead is entirely coincidental.

Lulu

ISBN: 978-0-6152-2067-3

Lobo Publishing
978 Peutz Valley Road
Alpine, CA 91901

VALLEY FEVER

Prologue

THE BEAR

THE BEAR

The creature struggled up and over the rocks. The bear was hurting from deep and life-threatening wounds, and he thrashed his mammoth hulk from side to side in a futile attempt to throw off the pain. All of its instincts drove it on, despite the suffering, on to the place of safety.

The cave was more than sanctuary, more than a place where life had regenerated through deep long sleeps and the birthing of cubs. It was dark and rank with known smells; a last stronghold against those who competed for survival in an icy world. The cave looked out on that which was unknown. Beyond the opening of this dark-channeled passage lay all danger. The mouth of the passage funneled and compressed any possible threat, focalizing and simplifying the need for decision. From this familiar ground, *Arctodus* would make the un-complex decisions in defense of its life.

This would be the last return from the last hunt. The short-faced bear had long been the most powerful of predators. But now there were new competitors, and their large size and very number gave them dominance in a world growing colder.

As the bear drew its heavy carcass wearily over the ledge, its fortress just within reach, the alarming scent of Grizzly suddenly battered the senses. *Arctodus* bear rose up on long hind legs and roared in anger at the unseen trespasser. Pain had turned to fury in the realization that its den was violated. From the mouth of the cave came a thunderous reply.

There was no time to plan a strategy, and there was no vantage point from which to execute it. Here on this precipice lay the stage for the extinction of a species. *Arctodus* bear looked to the entrance in time to see the giant Grizzly fill the black hole. The Grizzly didn't stop to guard its new claim, but came bellowing across the ledge, huge head baring yellowed teeth.

Rising to its full height, the Grizzly swiped at the air between them with massively clawed front feet.

In defiance, nurtured more by pain than tactical defense, *Arctodus* made its stand on the edge of the ice-shaled mountain. The air was cut with one flying paw and then another. Great slobbering strands of saliva flew from snarling mouths. And then a powerful front paw found its mark, crashing against the jaw of *Arctodus* bear. It reeled on one hind leg, seeking balance against the sky, and failing hurled over the edge and into the yawning wind.

***

Chapter I

WHERE TIME STANDS STILL

WHERE TIME STANDS STILL

Peter Caulfield was sure he'd die at the water fountain and, while he struggled to catch his breath, envisioned the headlines of tomorrow's campus newspaper, "Head of Archaeological Department, Last of His Kind, Found Dead at Watering Hole". Cynical humor did little to console the professor. After a decade of inactivity, you don't run the length of the campus without tempting fate, Pete told himself. He checked his watch, five minutes past five. Surely, she'd wait. Refusing the temptation of a long, cold drink, the Professor resumed a pace more fitting one his age and physical condition.

In the back of his mind was the nagging thought that this might be a question of another missed opportunity. How many did you get in one life, anyway? He really couldn't chance missing another, not and live with himself. Amanda Thearle would be waiting at the lab, waiting to ask him about Valley Fever and its infrequently discussed side effect, hallucination. Peter Caulfield might not, most likely did not, have the answers, but this time he was going to listen to the questions.

Valley Fever, Pete pondered as he walked briskly; the scourge of the Archaeology department and his own personal nemesis. He thought about the scorn he had dumped on his brother-in-law, Jerod, twelve years ago, when he had begun to understand what Jerod was driving at with his many questions about the disease. Certainly, Valley Fever hadn't haunted Pete then as it did now.

The risk referred to in the textbooks was primarily a respiratory infection caused by the fungus *Coccidioides immitis*. However, the fungal spores, concealed in southwestern soil, evidently carried more than this infectious disease.

Did it in Jerod Axsom's case? Well, he had asked Pete questions, and a few times since had sent tentative feelers into their conversation. He wanted to know whether Pete knew anyone with the disease who had hallucinations. He hadn't then.

But more recently one of his students had contracted Valley Fever on a class expedition, and his behavior had changed so radically after his supposed recovery, that Pete had been worried for his welfare. Steve Lake had suddenly been very interested in everything about Native Americans, to the point of seeing Native images in rock formations. At first Pete had passed it off as a vivid imagination. Later he wasn't so sure.

Steve had come to the lab one late afternoon looking for him. Except for a janitor and a professor or two, there was usually no one in the west wing of the Science building at this time of day. Pete had found himself thoroughly absorbed in the difficult reconstruction of a Native skull, when an unexpected footfall broke his concentration.

"Professor Caulfield, may I speak with you a moment?"

And because he really was tired and in need of resting his eyes from the tedious work, he offered his student a chair and with noticeable relief asked, "What's up?"

The innocent face before him looked pained and weary. Pete hadn't noticed the change in Steve and he questioned his own awareness. It had always been important to him that he oversee his students' welfare. He knew the stresses of academia, and still remembered his own youthful struggle to balance finances and studies. Pete was prepared to counsel.

"I have to talk to someone, someone who will understand." Steve's voice had faltered, but an underlying fear emerged to prod him on.

Once Steve had assured himself of a compassionate listener, an incredible story spilled forth. He confessed to experiencing hallucinations. In these "trips," as Steve referred to them, he had suddenly found himself in a Native settlement. There was an attempt at communication between a Native woman and his self, but before he could understand or accept what she was trying to say ... and her pleas were desperate enough that she reached out with a crone-like hand to clutch at his clothing ... Steve had panicked, fighting his way back to this world.

Steve was obviously terrified. He hadn't slept, because he was afraid of losing control and again beginning this slippery slide – his exact words -- to another world. Pete had stopped himself just short of asking Steve if he was using drugs. There was something so sincere and intelligent and even innocent in the boy's eyes, that he knew better. So he listened patiently, genuinely concerned for Steve's physical, if not mental, health. And at the end of the conversation found he had nothing to offer, nothing that his mind could accept or validate, anyway. Only later did he face it. There was nothing in Steve's story that quite meshed with Pete's more conventional view of the world.

When the dean had called to inform him of his student's suicide, Pete had sat paralyzed while the receiver hummed its one-note monotony of broken connections. The guilt had been insufferable, and he had forced himself to act. It had taken time for him to understand exactly how that would be possible.

Pete found that his first courageous act was to allow his mind to open. He recalled Jerod, his sister's fiancé, and his questions. Replaying the scenes from memory he saw how, in the beginning, he had shut down the intimacy necessary for Jerod to confide more. Tentatively, but sincerely, he had tried to mend fences. He hadn't put that much effort in the task before his own curiosity took over and became his motive to listen. Jerod must have recognized the acceptance of truth, because he began to share his story in the same measured pace that Pete found necessary to digest it.

Pete's stride lengthened, exaggerating his height. A student walking in the other direction, familiar with the professor's large frame, would have wondered what possible reason there might be for such hurry. "Steady as a rock" and "solid as granite" had been the terms of reference and the point of puns when students and faculty alike talked about the paleontologist. Few would ever believe that a supposedly innocuous disease had struck fear in the professor's heart. Few would guess how shaken was his foundation.

Pete found himself entangled in putting together a giant jigsaw puzzle. The latest key puzzle piece had accidentally surfaced when he learned of a student at the University, Amanda Thearle, who had also journeyed via a Valley Fever hallucination. The student was majoring in Education with an emphasis on Native American studies. It was Amanda's class's attendance to view a film on Valley Fever in Pete's lab that brought her to him. The sophomore had asked Pete whether hallucinations were one of the symptoms, because the film hadn't discussed it. That question had prompted the professor to ask Amanda for this, admittedly, unscientific meeting.

As Pete crossed the lawn, he felt beaded perspiration line his brow and drop by drop fall where they were caught in the net of his bushy eyebrows. He pulled out the handkerchief to wipe his face and graying, red beard. His heart was pounding and he realized exercise alone did not explain these symptoms. He was nervous. The thought of this encounter had filled him with anxiety, but there ahead the girl was waiting at the door to his lab, and perhaps there was his opportunity for atonement.

She was very pretty in the way California girls were supposed to be pretty, tan and slender, with blonde trailing hair. Arizona had its share of beauties, too, Pete knew. As he drew closer and she turned in his direction, Pete immediately noticed what set her apart from the others. Self-consciously, the young woman brushed a lock of flaxen hair away from her face, revealing the most intense brown eyes on which Pete had ever gazed.

"I hope I haven't kept you long," Pete said between breaths.

"No, I only just arrived." She smiled gently, and for a moment her dark eyes warmed.

Pete unlocked the door and followed her into the room. He clicked on the light and a series of fluorescent overhead lights illuminated the room. The large laboratory was under a constant veil of dust that Pete and his students tolerated, because no amount of the janitor's attention ever improved it. High windows lined the far wall above a countered cupboard, and free-standing steel shelves that crisscrossed one end of the room groaned under the weight of thousands of fossils and rocks.

Amanda ignored the stool Pete offered her and casually walked over to the shelves. "You said on the phone that you know of others who've experienced hallucinations with Valley Fever. Is that right?" she asked.

The professor appreciatively took a stool for himself, and sat at the large work table in the middle of the room. A thin layer of the earth's crust covered all the in-process projects lying on the gray surface. The color and life were gone from rocks and bones alike and Pete eyed them with renewed suspicion.

"Yes," he answered. And because he didn't want to play games this time, added, "Others have had troubling experiences, and because of theirs, so have I."

Amanda stood staring at the objects on the shelves. The student ran a tentative finger across the dust and Pete felt the gesture begin to resurrect her past. She turned around and faced him, smiling wanly.

"Bears were the source of my trouble, you know? It was the bears who took me there ... to Golthlay and The People," she said.

"Golthlay?" Pete's eyes left her idle fingers, focusing intently on her face. "Do you mean Geronimo?"

"Yes, one and the same."

This can't be, Pete thought. But he fought the impulse to inject his alarm and fell silent. Amanda had moved to the window and her gaze was on far-off phantoms. Pete was certain that whatever was in her field of vision still eluded him.

"You know it would help if I could just get over the worst part," she said wistfully. "You know, the hallucination itself."

"However you want to do it, and whenever you're ready," Pete encouraged her. "There's no hurry here. This is the place where time stands still."

Amanda sighed. He had obviously misunderstood, but she took in a deep breath and began again.

***

"I woke up in the middle of the night, or I guess I woke up. It felt more like entering a nightmare. I know I felt terrible. Being only seven years old, I most likely had never experienced feeling terrible or sick, but it was more than that.

"Looking back, I know I was nauseous, my head pounded, and I felt weak, but there was something else. Things were not as they should be. Everything was different and that was making me sick! But at the time I was just scared and called out for my father."

Pete thought it interesting, how detached she had become, reflecting on the experience almost in the third person.

"The first day was kind of a blur. My parents came in the room and I could see they were very concerned. I must have been a frightening sight, you know, the rash and all? They actually took the mirror down off my dresser. We went to the doctor's office and he confirmed I had Valley Fever.

The trip over there was hell, I remember. But, as I said, the peculiar part was my knowing that the symptoms were not the cause, that Valley Fever was not the cause. It was just the effect. It's amazing. I was just a little girl, but I knew that."

"Anyway, pretty soon, the next day I think, the strange stuff began. It was quiet in the house and very cool and still in my bedroom. I was all bundled up in my bed because I was chilled, which had to be strange because it was May in Tucson. I remember my dog, Slouch, was lying on the rug by my bed. He was always with me."

"I began to hear mutterings, low complaining, sort of like nagging voices, except I couldn't make out what they were saying. There was this indistinguishable quality to the voices, and they seemed to come from within my head as much as outside of me. The voices caused my ears to itch and in a peculiar way even my brain."

Amanda stepped away from the window and restlessly began to walk the narrow passageway between the worktable and the first shelf. The nineteen-year-old seemed mesmerized with the dust of antiquity.

"This went on hour after hour, day after day. I'm not sure how many days. Much of this is a blur to me, or maybe I'm blocking. At some point I began to think of the voices as the bears. Whether it was a need to focus on their source, or my own stuffed animals sitting about the room, or -- I still don't know." Amanda ended, apparently exasperated.

"It looks like you've done your share of analyzing, too," Pete said. He found himself comparing her need to understand the nature of her experience to Jerod's attempt to do the same.

Amanda's eyes followed the shelves surrounding Pete Caulfield's lab and momentarily rested on the fossils labeled *Arctodus* Bear.

"Anyway, when I began to hear the bears I was living with Golthlay and the Apaches. Sort of a cue; I would hear the bears muttering and then I was somehow transported. At first I was terribly frightened, but I began to adapt. It seemed as though I lived with them a long time, certainly longer than the time of the hallucinations."

Amanda's face brightened. "A lot of my time with The People was wonderfully exciting ... like the horses and mules ... and the children. Oh, -- and especially the dances!"

Amanda whirled around to face him, her lithe body accentuating her mind's mobility. "It's strange confiding in you like this. I can't even talk to my mother and father about it. It's too painful for them. I guess it was a hard time for all of us." She was silent a moment and then continued.

"When I became sick, I mean sick over there ... with the Apaches, it was worse than being sick here. I think I was dying and had sort of accepted it." Amanda's eyes glistened as she forced herself to relive the experience.

"Golthlay asked the shaman to save my life, but the shaman wasn't certain he could help me. His powers had diminished. I suppose because he was an old man. But he asked the Mountain People to restore his powers and they did. They gave him the strong power of the bear, and when the shaman returned, Golthlay took me to the shaman's wikiup where they performed the healing ceremony. The power of the bear was passed to Golthlay, and I was healed."

Amanda ended her story suddenly and simply, and it took Pete a moment before he realized she was through.

"Do your parents know all of this?" Pete asked.

"Oh yes, they must. They permitted the ceremony! And yet it doesn't explain the time frame. You know ... all of the events in a different time and place? Only hallucinations explain any of it. So that's why we don't talk about it, my parents and me."

Pete thought about this. Hadn't he done the same thing? Steve's tale, or plea for help, was answered with a convenient label. One in which compartmentalized the information that neither he nor Steve had been able to grasp. "Hallucination" tidied it up a bit, by removing it from Pete's consciousness and conscience. But for others like poor Steve, young, vulnerable, and perhaps because of his very innocence, it was impossible to separate it from himself by calling it hallucination.

So this child, Amanda, had grown with her secret intact. She knew. She was and is conscious of her memory. She has not lied to herself to please others with conventional memories of childhood. She has just kept it to herself, until now. The thought was mind boggling. He remembered Socrates' words, "To thine own self be true". An entirely exaggerated meaning in its definition, Pete thought.

"Did you ever think about the possibility of a regression? That, perhaps you had lived in this Apache tribe in another life, and were now reliving a part of it?" Pete asked.

Amanda's eyes widened, but she spoke with conviction. "I know it's true. Now you are the second person to know it is true."

***

Pete locked the lab door and listened to the click of his own heels' echo as he walked down the hall. He pushed open one of the large double doors and exited into blinding sunlight. It was brighter somehow, and the granite steps merrily reflected the fractured light. The campus lawn rolled out before him green and cool, and the late afternoon shadows ran long shards in dark contrast across the grass. Pete walked quickly down the path leading to the faculty parking lot, his head buzzing with Amanda's last words.

No, he wasn't the second person to know. Amanda's reference to Golthlay and the bears had been the clues. Jerod had been interested in Golthlay. Jerod had found the fossil. Could it be? Could their stories be one and the same?

As he drove home, Pete's mind went back, reviewing the Jerod Axsom he had once known. Pete had written him off as an aging Vietnam veteran who seemed destined to live mired in his own haunting nightmares, prone to alcohol abuse, dysfunctional -- and incomprehensibly, his sister Linda's fiancé.

There had been changes since then, subtle enough on the outside. Jerod still wore his hair long, though neatly braided, dressed unconventionally, and was apparently quite content to be a loner. He and Pete's sister had married and bought an old ranch on the outskirts of town, becoming involved with the Native community out that way, and one Native in particular.

The relationship between the Native and Jerod had always been mysterious to Pete, and he knew it had something to do with the period of his hallucinations. This was about the time Jerod began to change, and Pete had first noticed it when they were working together on the construction dig.

But it had really begun before that, Jerod had said. It had begun with the child's exposure.

***

Chapter 2

EXPOSURE

The year nineteen hundred and ninety-one

EXPOSURE

The whirlwind plowed across the schoolyard, whipping the dust around the children. They laughed and choked as the game of tag became one of hide-and-go-seek. Mandy could barely see the vague outline of legs and arms reaching through the opaque clouds. Their game turned to hot excitement as dirt flew in the air. An arm shot wildly in front of her and Mandy swirled to escape its grasp. Giggles erupted to her left and she heard Susan shriek, "Mandy! Watch out!" It was too late. The second-grader tripped over someone's foot and sailed into a cloud of dirt.

For an instant Mandy thought it would be a soft landing, like the dreamlike watercolor shades that painted the schoolyard. But the ground came up hard and slapped her shins and knees, stinging and burning as the gravel worked its way under her tender skin. Her own sharp cry was lost on the wind, swept away with the screams of other children.

Mandy spat the dry dirt from her mouth and lifted herself on one arm. The whirlwind was spinning off crazily. Like a drunken sailor it raced across the schoolyard leaving those with whom it had brawled scattered on the ground. Susan pointed at Mandy's face and shrieked again. In spite of her bloody knees, Mandy laughed. Dirt had smeared their faces and only the hollows around their eyes remained clear. Mandy looked around and saw the other ghoulish faces emerge from the settled dust. The school bell rang and Mandy felt her knees burn.

Mrs. McDowell took one look at the disheveled seven-year-old and sent her to the nurse's office. Mandy's hair clung as damp corn silk on her brow and fell in tangled curls down her dirt-streaked neck. She walked stiffly down the corridor, one dress tie ripped and hanging. Her shoelaces dragged the floor behind her, but her knees hurt too much to bend and retie them. The school nurse eyed the filthy child and marched her into the bathroom to begin the task of washing away Arizona soil.

***

The Thearles hadn't lived out west long enough to take in stride the fierce desert sun and heat. They had moved to Tucson to escape the biting cold winters of Chicago; the cold wind that had blown off Lake Michigan piercing the thickest of winter coats and driving Dan's sinuses wild. He remembered the piercing pain as two red coals behind his eyes, the only warmth of winter.

Still, Ryann and he could not believe that the friendly Arizona warmth that greeted them in February had become this inferno of May. The temperature was well into the 90s, and holding. What would summer be like, Dan thought, disturbed by his own inability to adjust to the heat.

As he drove the Escort into the driveway, he saw Mandy struggling with the hose. She was tugging at the loops caught on a bush. A look of determination and a flush of anger on her face reminded Dan of his self.

He had been told frequently that his daughter took after him. The same fine, pale blonde hair, though his own was receding all too quickly. Mandy had her Dad's coloring, except for her eyes. She had Ryann's deep brown eyes; eyes that revealed more of the soul than his. That's what had attracted Dan to Mandy's mother; a pool of feeling, lying just beneath the surface of those eyes, ever ready to spill over and cleanse him with honest reality.

Dan turned off the engine and watched as Mandy kept pulling, stubbornly. The hose finally came loose and Mandy thumped to the ground pulling the great loops of twisted hose with her. Water spewed forth jerking the nozzle from her hand. Like a snake it slung here and there and finally pointed at the open window of the car.

It hit Dan in the face first. The cold water made him gasp and an expletive stuck in his throat, soon swallowed with the force of the gusher behind it. "Mandy!" Dan sputtered when he could. But now the hose had lost its power and fell limply to the dry lawn where the water ran on thirsty grass.

"Daddy! I'm sorry. I didn't mean it ..." Her voice trailed off and she began to cry. There behind her the western sky blazed its last glory of the day, illuminating her blonde head in a halo of light. There sat his daughter, both mischief maker and innocent, devil and angel.

Dan threw open the car door and flung sheets of water from his shirt. He had to admit, he'd cooled off some. In mock anger Dan scooped Mandy up from the lawn. But this game wasn't new and she was soon giggling.

They entered the house and it felt like a furnace. The swamp cooler was at its highest position night and day, but there was no relief. Dan was determined they were going to buy an air conditioner soon. No one, but no one, made it through a summer in Tucson without an air conditioner, Jack had said.

Jack Owens was Dan's shared ride to the plant, where they both worked. He was also Dan's guide to western living, warning him about scorpions and other wildlife wonders.

He found Ryann in the kitchen making a salad. His barefoot wife easily crossed the tiled floor and lifted her face to kiss him. Ryann had told him that the only relief from the heat was the cool clay tiles, and regretted that they couldn't have bought an old adobe home instead of the frame and stucco. There hadn't been time. When the engineering position at the plant was offered to Dan, he had sent a hurried telegram of acceptance. Ryann, Mandy, and he had giddily made plans to leave behind Chicago's winter without a thought to future housing. They agreed that the dream home would come later and he vowed it would be adobe.

Dan looked approvingly at the woman he married. Ryann was still very much the girl he met in college. With her long legs and cut-off jeans she hadn't changed a bit. Only smarter, he thought.

She smiled up at him wickedly and asked, "What was all that yelling about? What are you two up to?"

"The hose got Daddy all wet. But see, he's dry now," Mandy said matter-of-factly.

"Well, Slouch isn't!" Ryann would have added more, but the Airedale, who had slipped in the door behind Dan and Mandy, decided this was a good place to shake off the excess water. Mandy and Ryann tried in vain to cover themselves with their hands. In disgust, Ryann showed the dog out the kitchen door.

"Really, Mandy! That dog could live just fine outdoors."

"He's my best friend, Mommy." Mandy answered with such solemn sincerity that there was little doubt of Slouch's continued freedom.

The dog had been a sore point with her parents. His coming out West was their concession to their daughter's adjustment to a new environment and neighborhood. Slouch had come with them from Chicago, the entire 3,000 miles -- in the car. Dan was resigned to the Escort smelling forever like a kennel. More than once Dan had been tempted to just leave the dog behind at a rest stop. The frequent stops for gas, food, and facilities had tried his patience, and each time Slouch had to be put on a leash and given his freedom. Dan could still see himself stumbling behind the dog on some darkened highway, pleading with him to do his "business" so that they could get under way. Slouch would happily nose among the bushes certain that he was expected to blaze a new trail west.

Ryann and Dan had bought the puppy when Mandy was three. It was Dan's answer to their one-child family. Slouch was their other child. Slouch began his pitiful whine, as if to remind him.

"Wait 'til he dries off, Mandy. It won't hurt him to be outside for awhile."

"Okay, Daddy. I was in a twister and had to go to the nurse's office today," she answered brightly, her best friend immediately forgotten.

"She means she fell on the school grounds and banged up her knees again," said Ryann, shaking her head.

Amanda Marie Thearle had begun that stretching period of youth when the ground and her body met more often than not. She was still in the beginning stages of learning to ride her bike, and had destroyed the mailbox and several lawn chairs in the process. It was little wonder that she would sometimes complain that her legs hurt at night when Dan tucked her into bed. Growing, even living, was a hazard of being seven years old.

"That's why I have all these Band-Aids!" Mandy said proudly.

***

Ryann prepared their three plates with cold cuts and salad, and directed Mandy to help her carry their dinner and utensils outside to the patio where there might be some relief from the heat.

The back yard was good-sized compared to those of newer homes. It was a deep lot with grown trees in this older neighborhood of Tucson. Dan compared it to the homes in the tracts he passed on the way out of town to the plant. Those homes stood side by side on lots that seemed ridiculously precious when their small size was compared to the desert that sprawled out beyond them.

And there were the trees; someone, long before them, had the foresight to plant the shade trees. Cottonwoods, tamaracks, and palms graced the yard with their large boughs, reducing the temperature on even the hottest days by 10 degrees. While the sun's last rays still baked the front of the old white stucco house, here in the back yard cool air flowed under the growing sentries. It was a respite from a day of coping with temperatures and tempers.

Dan leaned back in the lounge chair with his hands behind his head. He breathed deeply and sighed his approval. They had eaten the light supper, and Ryann had gone back in the house to refill their ice tea glasses. Mandy was swinging on the swing that Dan had made, pushing her brown sturdy legs high in front of her, stretching for the sky. Dan saw his daughter always reaching beyond herself, and he recalled her stubborn determination the day she took her first steps.

Thirteen months was perhaps a bit older than the average toddler, but Mandy made up for lost time when she learned to walk. Dan could still see the look of surprise on her face when she had fallen forward after the first few steps. The fact that her first try ended with a fall and a bump on the head, didn't deter her. She screamed in rage more than hurt, and pushed herself back up on teetering legs to begin again. Ryann and he still talked about that day. Nothing would stop Mandy, not repeated falls and bruises, not warnings of caution or even sympathy. She plowed ahead, recovering from her tumbles a little faster each time. By the end of the day her erratic first steps had become a run down the hallway. They had put her to bed that night, black and blue and completely exhausted.

Dan was still in awe of parenthood. This entity, Mandy, came into their life, a blend of Ryann and himself, yet with a separate will. He had never quite adjusted to the miracle of it all. She was always presenting him with a new challenge to his thinking. He hadn't realized that he could grow so old and stuffy so quickly. She was there to remind him; his own key to an open mind, with her little foot stubbornly in place to keep the door open.

He thought of her statement the other night. She had just marched in the back door, with her wet tennis shoes sloshing mud on the kitchen floor. Ryann had reprimanded her sharply, sending her back out to leave her shoes on the porch, when Mandy said, "But the last time I was here I never saw my shoes again!"

"What are you talking about?" Ryann asked. "You've got them on."

"No, I mean a long time ago. I had to be barefoot," Mandy quietly insisted.

Dan had raised his head from the newspaper and looked curiously at first Mandy and then Ryann.

"What do you mean, honey?"

When Dan looked back again Mandy had joined Slouch outside the kitchen door, her protest obviously forgotten as she chattered away to a willing listener.

There was something strangely familiar about her remarks, and since that night Dan had sifted through memories of a life made richer, as well as problematic, since Mandy was born. Her kindergarten teacher had said she was precocious, but they had already known that.

Even before Amanda Marie Thearle was born, Ryann and Dan had agreed to allow their daughter normal development. They had witnessed their friends' hyperbolic attack on child rearing and the resulting neurotic children they were raising. Dan couldn't even stand to be around some of them. The emphasis was on exaggerated intelligence, with all of the other human qualities ignored, or worse yet, smothered; Tracy Owens, for instance.

Jack and Lisa Owens were raising their children, Tracy and Thad, with all their own yuppie values firmly entrenched in their children's psyches. Brains and intelligence existed for the purpose of acquiring things. The process itself was not applauded; the discoveries along the way were not heralded. There was no wonder in the universe; there were just the yuppie "toys".

Tracy was forever showing and gloating over her latest toy. Her values so mimicked her parents that she was dressed like a miniature Lisa. The last time Dan and Ryann had invited the Owens over, he opened the door to greet Lisa and Tracy in their look-alike mini skirts and pulled-to-one-side pony tails. And there, clutched in Tracy's hand, was her Barbie doll dressed to make it a threesome. Dan had felt instant embarrassment for Jack, as if in some strange way the "threesome" had emasculated his friend. If Dan's face reddened, Jack never noticed as he marched, booming, into their living room carrying Thad. And then Dan noticed their trendy Nike's with matching fluorescent green shoelaces.

Maybe he was making too much of extraneous behavior. Still, Dan was much more comfortable with his real world daughter who skinned her knees and slept with her dog. Mandy lived to explore. Her curiosity constantly drew her parents into her life. When she had a question about a bug in the yard, she could hardly refrain from interrupting Dan's conversation with a neighbor. She tried. You could see it in the way she squirmed and the contortions her face went through, but all of this same body language said I need to know, I must know. That desire to know was the single most important reason Dan adored his daughter.

And she was that much more precious because she was likely to be his only daughter, their only child. The unspoken words between Ryann and Dan were always there as they shared their daughter's life.

Ryann brought their tea glasses back to the picnic table and sat down beside him to witness Mandy do her best to fly from the seat of the swing.

Dan studied Ryann's face, the soft glow on her high cheekbones just barely visible in the last light of day. He could not make out her expression, but knew it from memory. Her eyes would have turned soft with affection, belying their blacker depths that could turn as cold and forbidding as Lake Michigan on a blustery day.

He thought of such a day more than four years ago, when he sat in old Dr. Sullivan's waiting room. Nervously, Dan thumbed an issue of *Arizona Highways*, while decisions beyond his control were being made about their life. Birth control was suddenly a cruel joke. All this time they had postponed having that second child. The boy Dan wanted, he had to admit, until other decisions had been found, such as better employment and a more hospitable environment for his sinuses. "Who's in charge here, anyway?" Dan found himself thinking.

The nurse appeared and cheerfully ushered Dan into Sullivan's office. Ryann was sitting in one of the two stiff-backed chairs facing the doctor's desk. She seemed smaller, less confident than when they had first arrived. And then Dr. Sullivan said the words that shrunk him as well. Ryann had a tumor. They would operate immediately. They would face on the operating table any prognosis for future conceptions or pregnancy. "They" held Ryann's very life, and therefore his own in their hands.

Another child was suddenly the last thing on Dan's mind. They could take the playpen, as guys referred to that mysterious female organ, the uterus. Leave him his woman. This life or death issue hit Dan squarely between the eyes and for some moments blinded him with its stunning blow. He vaguely remembered shaking the doctor's hand and fumbling for Ryann's coat as they left his office.

When they were home in the warmth of their bed, he held her head and rocked softly as they wept together. As the pain and fear subsided, Dan became the strong one, reassuring his wife, setting the tone for this new found courage that would help them meet head on life's crises.

Certainly they had. Ryann had lost her "playpen," but they had their Mandy. Slouch nosed underneath Dan's hand as it lay on his knee, and he whined as if to remind him, you have me, too.

***

Sometime in the middle of the night the wind picked up. The desert began to shift its sand and the fine silt found its way through the cracks and windowpanes of the old house. Dan remembered hearing the creaks and groans of the huge tamarack that grew just outside, behind the water cooler. It woke him and he got up to take a better look from the living room. On the inner wall he saw the moving shadows of the tree's thrashing branches -- an eerie display of dancing antlers made possible by the full moon.

He checked on Mandy and found her sound asleep, one arm draped across her dog. Slouch raised his head, but Mandy never heard her father quietly close the door.

***

Chapter 3

THE CAPTIVE

THE CAPTIVE

The holy man had exited his sweat bath and huddled close to the fire, but apart from the others. He had gone through the ritual necessary to insure the safety of the raiding party. His prayers and singing done, he now laid out his blanket and still did not prepare to sleep for many hours. Instead, the shaman looked to the heavens and his thoughts flowed up among the stars, searching for the familiar configurations that would mark his journey. The beckoning freedom of the open black night above his head swallowed his reaching mind, leaving his curled body to lie on the cold earth next to the dying embers.

***

The raiding war party had ridden long and hard. Their intent had been to attack the few ranches that followed the gully below. This would be their revenge for the killings by the cavalry and the push that had driven their band to the caves. A larger purpose would be to bring back food and goods to their people whose own stores of food, blankets, and horses had been depleted.

There were nine of them, including the leader and the shaman. They had been riding five days and their six remaining horses were worn, but the men were encouraged when they looked down from their rocky ledge and saw the corral.

Several of the younger braves were on their first raid. These uninitiated, inched along the ridge on their bellies to have a better view of the homestead. For those without a horse, the dream became tangible. The dozen horses in the corral contentedly grazed on the brush the rancher had thrown over their fence for feed. The Natives had maintained their silence, the wind was in their favor; the conditions were almost perfect.

They waited patiently for the rancher to return to the house. It was almost a certainty that only he and his family lived in the barren structure. There would be little resistance and for this reason the leader intended that they would take no more than what was necessary. They would kill the man, of course.

It was almost dusk, a favorable time to move undetected. Color was leaving the earth and the war party moved out unseen among the rocks. Those braves on foot and horseback picked their own way down the mountain to the valley floor. It was a scattered approach, seemingly without a plan, but their direction came from years of actual raids and, for the youngest, from childhood games of mock wars.

There were no words between them nor would they call to each other unless their lives were in certain danger. To call each other by name would bring a worse fate to the war party. Signals were given to the experienced braves so that messages were passed on to direct each man's placement.

Once they reached the bottom of the arroyo they tied the horses to several scrub oaks and proceeded on foot. A soft light was coming from the windows of the farmhouse. It would be the family's meal time and most likely the only hour the oil lamp would be used. Four of the warriors made their way to the house, splitting up to surround it. The other five would take the horses, hopefully leading several with the others tethered behind them.

The leader and one other had rifles, rare commodities in this war party. Both guns would be used in confronting the inhabitants of the house. In place now, they waited for the leader's signal and when it came they burst forth as one.

The wooden door flew open and a woman shrieked. There were two men at the table and the older one rose quickly to reach for his rifle that hung above the hutch along the wall. In the same instant an explosion of fire hurled him against the hutch, sending its small doors banging open and closed. The man's blood flew amongst the broken crockery.

And now the second gun moved to the younger man, but the woman had thrown herself in front of him. Both of them were killed in the same instant and the war party's leader assessed his bullet's toll.

The oil lamp had spilled its fire across the table and onto the wooden floor. In the fast approaching darkness the brilliant flames reached out and licked the few remaining pieces of furniture. In this brief moment the leader recognized that there was only a girl child left. She was standing rigid; her brown eyes huge in fear, while the light from the growing fire danced off her golden hair.

This was not as it was supposed to be. They had not intended to orphan the child, only prevent a witness who could threaten the security of the raiding party, or worse yet, their people's camp in the caves. The leader silently motioned for the others to gather the supplies for which they had come. They must work fast, there was no guarantee the fire wouldn't be seen from a distance.

Flames were trailing up the homemade curtains on both windows, and the hissing and cracking of the fire was growing louder. The warriors swept pots into the open blankets, gathered the gun and ammunition, and tore several pieces of jewelry from the body of the woman. No one looked at the child. There was no need to acknowledge her existence as she stood silent and removed from reality. The fear in her eyes had turned to a veil of indifference, and though she couldn't have been more than three she had already removed her self from life.

The warriors had turned to leave, and their leader searched the room one more time for anything of value that could be traded. His eyes fell on the girl and he made his decision then to take her with them.

Virginia Spiegler didn't protest when the brave grabbed her roughly and threw her over his shoulder. She didn't say a word until they were outside and she saw her new high-top button shoes sitting on the front porch, neatly placed there and waiting for her return.

"Shoes! Shoes! Shoes!" she yelled. But this was to be one of the last words in English that Virginia Spiegler would utter. She would never again say her name, even though that very morning her mother had coaxed her at length, and she had finally managed to repeat the five syllables in a row.

The raiding party retreated across the arroyo, joining the others who now had the horses roped and waiting at the corral. They were pleased to discover that some of the supposed horses were mules, and they spent precious minutes packing the goods that they had carried from the house. The child, too, was tied across the front of the leader's horse. One more stop was made at the well to refill their water carriers. They then left the homestead site where the burning house would soon light the southern sky.

In the darkness the band moved slowly, picking their way to higher ground, away from the fire that interfered with their night vision. Here, there was light enough from the stars, though a waning moon would appear at a later hour. They found their way amongst a mountain of glowing rocks and boulders.

Golthlay looked at the child lying face down across his horse. Her tangled mass of blonde curls made him think of the yellow ore so coveted by the white man. If there was value in this color, then the child, too, would be of value. He assured himself that his decision had been correct, as he remembered the stoic skepticism on the shaman's face. The raid had been fruitful, he was certain of that. This many horses and mules alone, justified the raid.

With the sacks of grain and seed tied to the mules and the other stores they carried back to the caves, Golthlay thought he might allow the shaman his Mountain Spirit Dance.

The Chiricahua clan lived up in the sacred mountain caves that The People now used when running from the soldiers. The real purpose of the caves was to store their religious paraphernalia, especially that of the Gan dancers. This was where their people in former times looked to the top of the mountain and watched the Gans descend. These were different times, and though their lives had always been hard, they ran now from the United States soldiers, as well as the Mexican army. There had been no plans for the Mountain Spirit Dance. Instead they waited for the returning war party and the next plan of their leader Golthlay.

In the hour that the moon appeared, Golthlay instructed the men to make camp. There would be no fire because their safety could not be assured until several days' distance was between themselves and the ranch. The leader took the sleeping child, covered in buckskin, and laid her close to him for warmth. She had not cried on the hard ride, and he found this remarkably unlike the other white children that he had seen. He could not know of Nature's merciful gift of detachment to those who suffered from such trauma or shock. The yellow one was quiet and that was accepted as a sign of respect. All the more reason, he thought, to allow her to live.

***

On the third day they reached the stream. Its gurgling sound mingled with the wind in the pines and it became as laughter to the little girl. They rode parallel with the creek for some distance when the child, who now sat passively in a sitting position in front of Golthlay, began to hum to herself. Within her own world she was content and happy. The little melody that her mother had once taught her floated on the air above the stream and below the pines, a pure sound that belonged on this mountain just as certainly. The other warriors looked up surprised.

They stopped for a noon-day meal, the first on this hurried journey back to The People. Golthlay tore a strip of the dried deer meat that he carried in his food pouch, and handing it to the child he called her by her new name, Yellow Bird. The shaman had decided on this name as they rode, as it so aptly described the child's hair and voice. These, the first words anyone had spoken to her in the three days of her new life, settled immediately in her mind and she repeated them aloud. The leader seemed pleased and a smile crossed his face. The little one pointed at Golthlay questioningly. When he told her his name, she repeated it as well.

The braves filled their water containers at the running stream and drank their fill after allowing the horses to do the same. It was a beautiful spot at the water's edge. Summer was ending and the dried grasses made a comfortable place on which to lie back and stretch their bodies from the cramped riding position.

The daytime air was still warm at this altitude and it blew gently across the nearly naked bodies of the raiding party. It was easy to take this tranquil scene for granted, but Golthlay knew they had to leave it soon. They could not endanger themselves or their people by carelessly exposing their position to any army scouts. His instincts had served him well and he abided them now as he motioned for the braves to mount again. Yellow Bird would be his talisman for good luck, he thought, but he would continue to rely on the spirits that had guided him this far.

***

As they continued their climb in the mountains, the winding trail narrowed, precariously revealing the dizzying depths. Each man led his horse or mule and two others tethered behind, following in single file. Yellow Bird sat squarely on the first horse and looked out at the range to the east. High above her, at the very peak, stood two boulders side by side. The child pointed a small hand to the rocks, which marked an imagined passage to the sky. Her exclamation was one of awe, and Golthlay acknowledged its importance. This was the home of the Mountain People.

The caves of the Apache clan were far below the Mountain People, and it was with the permission of Life Giver that they hunted the land that was usually so rich with wild life. The Shaman took pollen from his medicine bag and sprinkled it to the east. It floated in the air that rose from their path, clinging to the mountainside in its ascent. Small particles caught in the child's hair and danced in the sunlight.

Along the trail there suddenly appeared other members of the clan. They were the men who guarded the camp. There were warm enthusiastic greetings and praise for a successful raid, as they followed the returning victors into the clearing.

Children approached the horses and mules, clapping their hands and merrily exclaiming their welcome. The women helped unpack the animals, falling greedily on the store of supplies. Still, it was divided in the Indian custom, to feed first the old and the children, for there was always a discipline present even in times of excitement, even the return of the raiding party.

Golthlay dropped the child down from his horse, instructing his wife to care for her. His own daughter, just a few years older than Yellow Bird, watched shyly. A group of children gathered to examine the white man's child. No taunting was allowed, as the woman took the child's hand and led her to their blanket.

Yellow Bird was not afraid; her interest was much too keen to allow for fear. She stood quietly while the woman took off her soiled dress and bathed her. Here by the little stream that ran at the foot of the hill, the women of the clan brought their vessels to carry water back up to the cave. They brought the smallest of children and supervised their bathing.

The water was icy cold and Yellow Bird shivered visibly, but she did little more than gasp when her head was doused to wash her hair. When her body was dried carefully, the woman pulled a soft buckskin shirt down over her head. The softness was reassuring and Yellow Bird became very sleepy. When they had walked back up the hill to the cave, her hand in that of Golthlay's woman, she returned to the blanket and immediately fell asleep.

***

In the dusk the child slept while the men of the clan gathered to discuss the raid and to plan the ceremony. The medicine man, several of the dancers, and others who would paint and dress them, left to prepare at a sheltered plateau higher on the mountain. They were careful to hide themselves from the tribe's women and children, for they would be impersonating the Supernaturals.

A story revealed the caution that must be exercised during the ceremony and warned of the consequences. Long ago a medicine man instructed everyone not involved in the preparation of the dancers to stay below. When they returned no one was to call to the dancers by name. A little girl disobeyed and was caught by the Mountain People. The shaman tried to hide the girl behind the dance fire, but the Mountain Spirits had replaced their impersonators in the dance. For three nights a Mountain Spirit, painted a different color, led the futile search for the child, but on the fourth night the Clown dancer found and slew the child.

The four-night ceremony that Golthlay had permitted the shaman to perform was for the purpose of extricating the illness that had afflicted some of The People. The sickness, or evil spirit, would be driven away by the Gan. It had become more urgent because there had been a death in their absence.

A young boy had died with the wasting, coughing disease. The tribal elders were displeased, as well as the boy's parents, that the shaman had not been there to attend him. They were further concerned that the war party brought back the girl. No longer having a permanent camp made the taking of hostages or captives an unwise move. Golthlay saw the

Mountain Spirit Dance as an appeasement to his people as well, as to the Mountain People.

***

On the rock ledge and out of view of the tribe, the shaman now prepared to instruct how the dancer's bodies were to be painted in the decorations of the Gan. The men who would be the dancers stripped to their skirts and moccasins and sat facing the east. The shaman blew smoke in each of the four directions and chanted a prayer that spoke of the relationship of the Mountain Spirits to the performers.

The painting began. Besides the regular Gan dancers, there were the Clown and Black One. The Clown was painted white and dressed only in a breechcloth and moccasins. He wore a scraped rawhide mask with large ears. His power was most important in sending away the "sick" spirit. But it was the Black One who was most feared. Anyone who touched him during the dance would be harmed, as he was there to keep everything bad away. He was the only dancer painted entirely black and without a headdress. Feathers sprung from the top of his mask, and he would be dressed in a woven skirt of yucca. Spruce would be tied to each arm and he would carry a spruce wand as well. The Black One would move silently during the dance, not mixing with the others.

Each of the Gan dancers was given an undercoating of greenish brown. A yellow snake was painted on each arm, the head reaching for the shoulder blade. Different designs in yellow were drawn on the front and back of the dancers. The first man had a yellow bear on his chest and a Gan of the same size painted on his back. The second man had a bear on his chest and a lightning bolt on his back. The third man had a zigzag of lightning bolts painted on both his front and back.

This event was an intense, solemn occasion, and the helpers carefully took from the cave the elaborate headdresses, known as chas-a-i-wit-te. These wooden framed head pieces were made of slats from Spanish bayonets and had attached painted symbols and decorations. They would be worn by the regular Gan dancers along with the blackened buckskin masks.

The medicine man beat on his clay drum and sang songs calling on the mountain spirits to give them endurance during the dancing. Once the body painting was finished they all ate a special meal that had been provided by their sponsors, the relatives of those who were the sickest.

It was nearly dark and time for the dancers to descend to the great fire below that was made to illuminate their dance. The shaman directed the dancers to form a line facing east, their headdresses in hand. They prayed asking to be blessed, then turned in a clockwise direction and called out to the Mountain Spirits. Each of the Gan dancers and the Clown spat in to their buckskin masks four times, made three gestures of putting on the masks and then pulled the masks over their heads. An owl flew out from a pine growing on the side of the mountain and soared without a sound parallel to the performers. It then swooped to the lower grove of oaks and disappeared.

***

The costumed dancers set out to walk single file down the mountainside. In the half light their head pieces seemed to float like grand candelabras above them. Clusters of wood pieces hung by leather thongs from the horizontal supports and the soft chiming sound that they made as they struck each other announced the coming of the Mountain Spirits.

Yellow Bird, aroused from her sleep, was spellbound with the pageant that was beginning. Little attention was given to the small girl and so she unobtrusively joined the other children at the fire's edge.

The representatives of the Mountain People entered the firelight where the Apache people had gathered, and the curing ceremony, the Cha-ja-la, began. The dancers were carrying long wands painted with blue lightning lines, and as they began to dance they emitted a strange whistling noise. They bent slowly to the right and then to the left, then forward and backward, until their heads were level with their waists. Then they spun around full circle, first on the left foot and then in the opposite direction on the right foot. The Gans thrust their wands in an imaginary way to dispel the evil spirits.

As the beating of the drums filled the air, a visual mystery unfolded. Light flickered off the dancers as they moved erratically and swiftly through the crowd. The sick were presented and the dancers took turns warding off their evil spirits.

The Clown, with his grotesque big ears, received the most attention. Silent, except when he delivered messages to the Gan, he followed the directions that the people gave him, making a fool of himself to the delight of all. It was his power that was the strongest in curing the sickness, and as he approached the ill, the women and children parted to allow him room.

In spite of the serious purpose of the dance, The People were satisfied with the return of the war party and their successful raid. It was a joyous time and yet they were ever conscious of the ritual. They were careful not to cry out names, even when they identified certain dancers.

The captive child was frightened. She was suddenly alone amongst a strange people. Though her mind had blocked the recent traumatic event in her life, her new caretaker was not to be seen. Her tears and sobs went unheard amidst the commotion of chanting and drums. She didn't dare leave the light of the fire, and she couldn't take her eyes off the swirling dancers. She feared exploring the mysteries of the darkened caves that lay beyond the light. There was only one person who was not a stranger to her, and though Golthlay was the murderer of her family, Yellow Bird looked frantically for his presence.

And then she recognized him. There he was, painted black, moving slowly by the fire. The other dancers kept a distance from him. His cloth mask did little to disguise his features, and his short, muscular body was easily recognized. The child, who had been quietly sobbing, now cried out "Golthlay!" as she stumbled to her feet and ran blindly to her protector. Yellow Bird repeated her cry and in the ensuing silence her words became distinct.

The People stood horrified as they watched her call their leader by name. The girl would bring the wrath of the Mountain People down on them. Midway across the clearing Golthlay's woman grabbed the child as she ran, spinning her around and into the folds of her skirts where her words became muffled. The woman led the child away quickly, but it was too late; her words had been heard.

***

Chapter 4

THE FIND

THE FIND

His patience was running out, a limited supply at best. Jerod dropped two more coins in the pay phone and re-dialed Linda's number. He heard the clicks and imagined his message pulses buzzing down wires, seeking the proper corridors, passing the rejected blind alleys, and speeding on to their preconceived destination. The final hiss of static stopped and there was a full three seconds of dead silence as he waited for the phone to ring at Linda's apartment, 120 miles away in Phoenix.

"Hello," she answered suspiciously.

"Don't hang up. Just listen to me a minute. Hear me out." When Jerod was fairly certain she wouldn't slam the receiver down again, he continued. "You gotta understand, Linda, it's just not that easy to get things going again."

"Oh you seem to have things going again, all right!"

She was still angry, but he could tell she had been crying. She sounded more vulnerable, more open to some reassurance on his part, willing something, anything, to take the hurt away.

"I'm going back to AA. It's not like its permanent or anything. So I had a few beers. I know I messed up, but this job has been a bitch with one holdup after another." Jerod hesitated a second to see if she would take advantage of the opening and when she didn't he continued. "You know I want you here, but until we get some regular pay I can't get an apartment for us. Pete's putting up with me. What can I say?"

His last statement hadn't come out in the form of a question, but Linda took the opportunity.

"I know, honey. I can put up with this ... really." Her voice had turned soft. "It's not the separation, though I miss you so much, but if you go back to drinking with all we've been through ... well, we just can't make it then."

Jerod thought of those years when alcohol was a way of numbing his "Vietnam jig," as he called it. He had been one of the walking casualties, hanging together with luck and something more. The something more being only recently discovered and identified. In those days there was no order to his life. He woke up and worked if he felt like it and most of the time he didn't. A wild look in his eye, disheveled long hair, and unwashed body didn't get him past the foreman on any job. But it hadn't mattered. To hell with them, he thought. He smoked pot and coaxed a haze of detachment to insulate himself from the world.

After some time on the phone they were listening to each other once again. They finished the conversation gently, assuring one another of their love. When Jerod put the receiver back on the hook he could hear the strains of "The Wichita Lineman" coming from the open doors of the convenience store. Yeah, he thought, as he saw the telephone poles follow the highway out of sight, even on this flat desert objects disappeared from sight. The wires had once again been severed and all connections were broken. But he had promised Linda she would be with him, and he with her. They didn't need a telephone, or even each other's presence. If they didn't know each other by now, the telephone wouldn't help. They would communicate with thought and something more.

Jerod Axsom went into the store to buy a Big Gulp, a pack of cigarettes, and some Rolaids. Though this was his lunch hour, he wasn't hungry. Maybe it was the phone call, or the blasted heat, or more likely last night's bash. The burly guy behind the counter yelled at the kid exiting the store to close the damn door.

"You'd think he paid for the air conditioning, huh?" he mumbled as he rang up Jerod's order.

Jerod read the thermometer hanging beside the cash register: 82 degrees and it actually felt cool. He'd better get back outside fast before he decided this was the good life.

The convenience store was three short blocks from the job site. Jerod drove past the elementary school, crossed the street, and pulled into the gravel driveway to park beside the other pickups belonging to his crew. He had just two others working with him on this job. They were excavating the site for the planned lower level parking area under the apartment building.

As was to be expected, the guys had become close. They were all some distance from home, and if Jerod hadn't been offered the spare bedroom at Linda's brother's house he would have shared housing with them. For several weeks they had hassled Jerod for not joining them for a beer after work. Was he too good for them? This was the underlying question, and he hadn't bothered to tell them that he was a recovering alcoholic ... in a new place, a new setting. Why had he decided to experiment with reality? It wasn't as if he hadn't dealt with his alcoholism, he had just thought it unnecessary to bring the information along like so much baggage.

And then yesterday everything had gone wrong. Equipment was breaking; the inspector hadn't shown. When the afternoon arrived and they still couldn't get things moving, Jerod decided to call it quits. The guys made their pitch as usual, and this time Jerod said yes. They had hit the bar about two in the afternoon, and somehow he had managed to drive the truck back to Pete's a good twelve hours later.

He had tied one on for sure. There was definitely no manageable tolerance in his repertoire. He vaguely remembered feeding the jukebox and watching the bar crowd change shifts and "outstaying" them all. When he had finally driven home and gained a noisy access to his bedroom, he saw Pete standing in the hallway in his polka dot shorts watching him, totally disgusted.

That mirrored image is to what Jerod awoke. Yeah, he had blown it. But how do you undo it? You don't. It would have just ended there, but Linda had called more than once while he was out, and the last time she unfortunately caught him just crawling into bed. She knew her man, and the slurred words had told her everything that Pete hadn't.

***

His stomach didn't feel settled, but his mind did. Jerod could forgive himself and was willing to get on with life, in particular, this job. The guys were finishing their lunch break on the tailgate of a truck. Several pieces of trash, wrappers, and an aluminum can blew out of the truck bed. Jerod reached to pick up the trash and the wind teasingly lifted them, sending them tumbling off across the lot. They came to rest at an excavated swath that would be foundation footings for the future underground parking area. Jerod heard snickers behind his back as he awkwardly chased the trash down the bank.

"Well, damn it, I've told you guys to watch your shit," he called out. He felt every bit the fussy environmentalist and at least a little foolish. The cut by the backhoe was fresh and something about the color and patterns in the earth caught his attention. He put his hand out to rub the lose dirt away from a lighter area and felt the smoothness underneath.

It was bone, he was pretty sure. Jerod called to Rick and Bill and they joined him as he began to chip at the sandstone around it. No one felt too healthy from the night before, and the two were perfectly willing to delay starting up the equipment. The men were not so much interested in what the hell Jerod was doing as they were in watching him from this shaded side of the bank.

The afternoon wore on and the shadows deepened. Though the inspector had finally come that morning and they had the go ahead for grading, all work came to a stop as Jerod became involved in his own private excavation. He had now extricated the piece that really did look like bone and several pieces of rock that were very strangely marked.

Jerod took off his shirt and his deep brown back soon glistened in sweat. The sun had been beating on him unmercifully, while the others stood or sat in the shadows. The men began feeling a little uneasy. They were paid by the day and this would be another half day of work for a full day of pay.

"Hey, Jerod! Don't you think we better hit it?" asked Bill.

"Yeah, I thought the guy you room with was the bone man. Jesus, Jerod, do we work or not?" Rick asked, restlessly.

"What time is it?" Jerod said, suddenly realizing the day was slipping away.

"Three thirty."

"Why don't you knock off. I'll pay for eight."

The crew didn't hang around to debate. Their energy had ebbed as they suffered the full impact of their hangovers. Within minutes they'd picked up their tools, secured the heavy equipment and drove their trucks off in a cloud of dust.

It was quiet with the guys gone, their jokes and verbal banter with them. Finally, it occurred to Jerod what this find of bones could mean to his schedule. Everything would be held up while some gleeful government agency determined if he had discovered stone-age man. There had been enough stops and starts with this job; he did not need a bureaucratic hang-up. Still, it was fascinating, and he wondered about the history of the area.

Jerod carefully wrapped the bone and rocks in his t-shirt and placed them on the passenger seat. Rick had inadvertently given him an idea. He would show the pieces to Pete, the paleontologist. This was his field of expertise, and Jerod was pretty sure he could trust Linda's brother not to blab it to the world, assuming he hadn't been too upset about last night.

***

It had been a little awkward living with Peter Caulfield and his wife Jenny. Jerod would have liked to rent an apartment for Linda and his self. Face it, Linda's job at the bank was paying the bills until such time as his excavation company would be solvent. The building boom was over and the Southwest had been hurt hard. He had left Phoenix when this opportunity in Tucson surfaced. You had to follow the work.

But his life-style was not really compatible with Pete's. Linda and he were a whole lot less conventional, coming and going as they pleased. He was grateful to Pete for the room, but could do without the watchdog.

They were concerned with his health, he told himself. He felt fragile under their scrutiny, and of course that was why they watched his every mood. The truth was he had not been very stable throughout his entire on-again, off-again relationship with Linda, and their stake had been with Pete's sister.

When Jerod arrived at home he found a note on the dining-room table. The Caulfield's had gone out for the evening to one of the many functions they attended, this one with friends from the museum. There was a steak defrosted in the refrigerator, and Jerod found he had worked up an appetite. He prepared himself a salad while the broiler preheated, his attention drawn frequently to the bundle he had deposited on the table.

Jerod unwrapped his shirt and took the bone and each rock and set them out separately at the far end of the table. While he ate his dinner he studied the designs and deep colors imbedded in the rocks. It was hard to describe his feelings. If he could, Jerod would have confessed a strange reverence and an uncomfortable feeling of trespass.

It was late when he cleaned up the kitchen. The house was quiet, except for the whir of the air conditioner. Jerod's concentration was unbroken as he deposited his dirty jeans in the laundry basket and turned on the shower. The cool water felt good on his sunburned back and he stood there, longer than usual, allowing muscles to relax and give up their wired reflex. When he dropped into bed it was only moments before he was asleep.

***

He had to rearrange the water pipes. This gray water would nourish the cactus if the pipes could release their precious water where they were planted. It hadn't seemed like a problem when he began, even though it was difficult walking in this sand. Jerod would lift a foot and the sand would spill into the funnel of his footprint and so the next step would not let him progress up the hill. He became impatient, and labored determinedly to get up the hill. Only, the sand was pouring down and around his feet just as quickly. He turned, looking to find another route up the dune, but when he moved forward other hills of sifting sand became unstable, sliding down and around his legs. He couldn't walk now. There was too much pressure on his legs, and still the sand kept rising like an incoming tide. He was close to panic and yet there was that instant when he felt he might control the situation if he stood absolutely still and allowed the sand to stop its slide. He was sweating now in immobilized fear. If this did not work and he called out, who would hear him? He watched each grain fall to rest against another and then sickeningly turn fluid with the weight of the sand behind it. The moment of control slipped with it and Jerod screamed his self awake.

When he opened his eyes he was sitting straight up in bed, a survivor amongst twisted sheets. He waited to see if he had wakened anyone, his mouth dry as cotton. Christ, what a nightmare. Had he screamed aloud? As moments went by and no one came bursting into his bedroom, he eased back into his damp pillow. But this wouldn't do. He had to get up, his throat hurt and he needed a drink of water.

As he stood at the sink looking into the mirror, Jerod thought about the wild-eyed reflection. Maybe he'd better get back to AA. His promise to Linda had been more to satisfy her than to have any real concern that his fall off the wagon was here to stay. Yet, looking at this forty-two year-old aging hippie was suddenly frightening. He couldn't afford to lose his grip at this stage of life.

Jerod drank long from the running spigot as he held his straggly long hair out of the way. His head was pounding and he took three Excedrin before returning to bed.

***

"Hey, what do we have here?" asked Jenny, motioning to Jerod's find on the table.

"I must have forgotten to put them away." Jerod was late and at this moment his only interest was a cup of coffee.

"Where did you find them, on the job?" Pete was wolfing down his usual high cholesterol breakfast of eggs, sausage and buttered toast.

Jerod's stomach took a flip as he watched Pete mop up the yolk on his plate with a piece of bread. He shakily poured his coffee and found a chair at the table. This is too long for a hangover, he thought. Jerod eyed Pete's ability to cope with the morning suspiciously. Linda's brother had always been amiable enough, but his manner implied his education was synonymous with authority.

"Yeah, I was curious. Maybe you can tell me about this stuff without bringing down the construction busters. That piece looks like bone, doesn't it?"

Pete had picked up the smooth piece that had first interested Jerod. He turned it over several times and said matter-of-factly that it was fossilized bone.

"So, like is it old, or what?"

"It would not be a fossil if it weren't old, Jerod." Pete answered in a patronizing tone that suggested he indeed was the elder of the two. Looking up at Jerod his bushy, red eyebrows puckered.

"What's the matter with your face? You've got a rash or something?"

Jenny padded around the table in her pink slippers and robe to take a closer look. She leaned over and examined him. "It looks like you've been in poison oak."

"Oh, it was probably something I ate." Jerod had enough. "Before I moved in, that is." He really had to get outside. The air was getting stuffy in here.

Before Jerod left he picked up the rocks off the table, leaving Pete to scrutinize the bone. He wasn't sure why they fascinated him more, but he held them close to his body, still wrapped in yesterday's shirt.

Jerod stopped in the hallway and looked in the mirror. Maybe he was allergic to alcohol. Now that was a good one. He laughed and it became a coughing fit. Jerod let himself out the door quickly before he had everyone's attention again.

He had only worked several hours when he realized he couldn't make it through the day. Jerod felt awful. He asked Rick whether he would take charge, and fumbled for his keys to the pick-up. No one was home when he returned. Setting the rocks down on the end table, Jerod fell weakly into bed.

When he woke the phone was ringing and although there was no extension in his room, from the bed he could see down the hallway the phone on the wall of the dining room. The phone rang urgently and it sent out expanding circles of sound, circles that he could see. Jerod tried to get up and couldn't. This was crazy, he must be dreaming, he thought. He was disoriented and maybe not fully awake. He lay there helplessly while the sound of the phone pulsed visibly filling the hallway with colors. He thought of the sound boxes that flashed acoustical color and thought it a great trick. His mind was giving him a light show. Well, lay back and enjoy it, he told himself. It can't go on forever. And it didn't.

In blinking to verify this bizarre scene, his eyes refocused on the rocks lying on the table beside his head. His shirt had fallen away, exposing them. Within inches of his face a black masked head stared back. Two eyes glared out from the torn holes in the cloth and sprouting from the top of the head was a cluster of feathers. The head was the rock, or the rock was the head, he wasn't sure. It hovered in front of him, undeniably real. Jerod was aware of the sound of hollowed wood chimes in his bedroom. A cool breeze swept over his body, and his skin began to crawl. He found his arms unable to move as he instinctively tried to reach for the blanket on his bed.

While Jerod fought with this reality, a slit in the mask that was obviously the mouth opened and spoke.

"I call on you, Great Spirit. Intervene!"

All of the rocks on the table began to vibrate in a rising tempo. Their tapping became louder and the pounding filled Jerod's ears, overwhelming the sound of chimes. The rocks were thrashing about the small table, beating savagely on its wooden surface. In helpless panic, Jerod tried to move. His arms were frozen against his side and his mouth formed a silent zero, as even his breath was paralyzed in his throat.

Then suddenly it was over. The rocks were only rocks and the inanimate objects fell still. The only sound was the phone that rang incessantly. Jerod rose from the bed, shaken, but in control of his body once more. He felt tentatively for the floor with his bare feet and finding solid footing made his way down the hallway to the phone.

"Hello," he mumbled.

"Jerod, is that you?" Linda's voice was like a clear morning, and Jerod found the fog begin to lift.

She had a thousand questions, and Jerod listened to her concerns, unable to reassure her, hardly able to assure himself. He looked down at his arms and saw the rash had spread, red and angry looking.

"Yeah, I'll see a doctor," he said, but he was determined to attend an AA meeting first. He had never experienced the D.T.'s before. Maybe this was it.

***

Chapter 5

AA MEETING

AA MEETING

Linda returned the receiver softly to its cradle. There was no mistaking it, Jerod was in trouble. She tossed her straight blonde hair back out of her eyes, and looked around to see if anyone had witnessed this disturbing call. Linda wasn't in the habit of using the bank's toll-free line for personal use, but something had told her to call her brother's house. Their "something more" was working, or at least it was for her.

In happier times she and Jerod would have laughed about their uncanny ability to reach each other without communication. She almost wished the "something more" wasn't working. There was this aura of dread she carried with her to work the last couple of days. Even the girls in the office noticed it. Pam had asked her if she had P.M.S., because if so, she had this special herbal tea that worked really well for her. Actually, Linda wanted something a good deal stronger, but felt the usual guilt when she thought about having a drink when this was most likely the root of Jerod's problem.

Jerod had taken *so* long to answer the phone. But why had she let it ring? When finally his voice came on the other end of the line, she felt a measure of relief. It was as if she had saved him from drowning, or worse. He had absolutely no explanation for being home in the middle of the day. He didn't even try to lie, and even stranger, he did not sound like he had been drinking.

She made up her mind to drive to Tucson tonight. They hadn't planned on getting together until next weekend, but Jerod sounded like he was over the edge, and it would just be better if she knew what was going on. Besides, Pete and Jenny really didn't have a clue.

Linda fought back the tears as she cleared her desk. It had been such a long battle, Jerod's recovery. And she had invested heavily. She was thirty-five years old and still hoping to settle down for the first time, while her girlfriends had children, and even second marriages. Like the banker she was, she questioned her investment of time and the paltry interest she had earned. Everything had begun to look so good for the two of them, and she hadn't minded carrying them while Jerod launched his business, but liquor had been the wild card. There wasn't a way that she could make this decision for him, but she definitely needed to know what it was.

***

Once Jerod was behind the wheel he began to settle down. He headed for the highway with his windows rolled down and let the dry Arizona wind sweep through the car. The clean, pure smell of orange blossoms followed the car's progress. He took a physical assessment and decided that his only complaint at the moment was this damn itch. But the air felt good and to get his mind off the creeping crud and the weird trip he had just experienced, he thought about where he was going.

It had been all too familiar looking up Alcoholics Anonymous in the yellow pages. Jerod found the listing for their central office, and found a meeting scheduled for two this Friday afternoon. The catch was that it was out of town, but maybe that, too, was what the doctor ordered. He needed some time alone.

The days of regular AA meetings had been over for some time. When the battle to recovery was one day at a time, and if he dared forget, he was reminded by those used-up faces seated around the table who took turns discussing their own time in hell. When, exactly, did he start taking it all for granted? A new business in a new city -- that was stress. Under times of stress you overlooked your weaknesses, made little of them. Jerod had begun to feel invincible and that was dangerous.

He located the small community church out on Canal Road, on the outskirts of Tucson. There was not much else out here, a rather run-down area with scattered houses and occasional livestock pens tucked behind them. Jerod approached a few Native Americans gathered in front of the church and asked them if this was where the meeting was held. They nodded, without changing expression, and moved away from the door to allow him entry.

Inside it wasn't much livelier. This was the community room where the church potlucks were held, only this afternoon it hosted recovering losers. Jerod noticed that they were predominately native, though a few wizened faces of aging ranchers spotted the smoky room. As inconspicuously as possible, Jerod took a folding chair from the stack against the wall and found a place at one of the long adjoining tables. He found himself adopting the serious demeanor of the other faces around the table.

It wasn't much like the meetings he had attended in Phoenix. In that urban setting there had been more young people, kids who had eventually found themselves on the streets dependent on drugs and booze. The ones who showed up at AA meetings had a slightly better chance of cleaning up than those who went to Narcotics Anonymous. There was still a rather romantic notion among these kids that using drugs and recovering from drug addiction was more "in" than using alcohol. The fact that addiction was the real issue was minimized in favor of hanging around your peers, expecting to be idolized as a savvy, street-wise dude.

The kids at AA would find their sponsors in a generation of older neophytes, those in their late twenties, early thirties. And they, in turn looked to those who, like Jerod, were veterans of life and war. This mixed package, plus a scattering of the loyal never-miss-a-meeting seniors had been the nuclei of the meetings that Jerod had attended.

***

Most of the seats were taken when a Native man entered the door. He was received with such attention and respect that Jerod knew his mentor role would place him at the head table. He moved quietly, greeting those along Jerod's side of the table. Jerod could see that he was probably in his fifties, though obviously well preserved in a small muscular body that was erect and moved easily. His hair was gray and hung in two neat braids close to his head.

The Native American extended his hand to Jerod and introduced himself. "Hello. My name is Bill. Welcome to our Canal meeting," he said softly.

He shook Jerod's hand and looked clearly into his eyes. Bill's skin was amazingly smooth, and though his eyes held ages in their black depths, his sculptured face was virile, yet strangely innocent. Jerod thought this supposed contradiction intriguing and was immediately mesmerized. Jerod introduced himself by the customary first name only and said that he was from Phoenix. Bill smiled and suggested he help himself to a cup of coffee before the meeting began.

Jerod hurriedly poured a cup of coffee, his hand shaking slightly, and returned to the table with odd anticipation. Bill presided over the meeting and in a distinct, but soft voice, led them in reciting the Serenity Prayer. He introduced the secretary and coffeemaker and asked those who were new to introduce themselves. Volunteers read from the Big Book, Chapter 5, the 12 steps of Alcoholics Anonymous, and then opened the meeting to speakers.

For the first time Jerod noticed that there were no women in the room. Though he had been to other meetings where only men had gathered, it was unusual for a meeting in the middle of the day. Maybe that explained why there was no "showboating". There just wasn't anyone of the opposite gender to impress.

Personal truth was the basis of the meeting as one man after another gave his AA story. Depending on the man's age, there was a corresponding portion of his story that was practiced and committed to memory, and it spilled forth in the style of its storyteller. But the need of this particular meeting brought the men to the point of exploration when they were speaking impromptu, discovering their way as they spoke. How were they handling their road to recovery? How did they feel that day on the job? Or what did they do to find a job? Were they reconciled to the wife and kids leaving? How did they manage the reunion with a grown child who had been the alcoholic's victim?

The road to self-discovery was an exhilarating stimulus to those around the table, and the room came alive as souls were stripped of the masks they wore outside. There was laughter and there were tears, as there had been both in the life of each man. There was no disrespect shown to another at the table, no matter what the confession or humiliation. Through it all, camaraderie grew among them and comforted those who had been lost.

Jerod had raised his hand quite naturally when moments had passed and there were no others asking permission to speak. Bill acknowledged him and Jerod began.

"Hi, it's good to be here. I'm a ways from home, but I guess home is where the meeting is." There were a few knowing laughs across the room as everyone felt more at ease with the stranger.

"I would have gone to my group in Phoenix for my fifth "birthday" in November, but its not gonna happen." Jerod had their attention. "No -- somewhere along the way I thought that in another time and place I wouldn't be me -- I wouldn't be me, the alcoholic. I guess I thought that if no one recognized me, didn't know my past, that somehow my past didn't exist.

"Well, I blew it. Two days ago I fell off the wagon; tied one on that was a humdinger. I've been suffering ever since. For two days I've been going through the usual questions. I've got a girl in Phoenix. We've planned on getting married. I've started a grading company. It was going okay. And then in one stupid move -- to deny my own alcoholism -- I threw it all away!"

Jerod was looking straight at Bill, fixing his attention on those ageless eyes.

"Today, I realize just how far I've drifted, and I think I'm losing it." His voice broke, and he momentarily struggled to continue. It took all the courage he could muster to go on, but when he looked up into the Native's eyes he felt stronger.

"I found these rocks and bones on the job site, see. They were really interesting, so I brought them over to the house where I'm staying. But I've been feeling lousy since the other night, and I came home early today to sleep it off. When I woke up I was hallucinating. D.T.'s, I guess. One of the rocks on the table beside my bed was wearing a mask and talking to me! Jesus! Well, to make a long story short, that's why I'm here." Jerod was embarrassed, but he got to the point. "I realize now that this was the lesson. I can't expect a disguise to change reality. I am an alcoholic and that doesn't change just because I'm in another town. It doesn't change because I *pretend* to be what I'm not! And, well, I'm glad to be here. Thanks for letting me speak."

Jerod sat back in his chair, suddenly exhausted and relieved that it was over. There was applause from the men around him and a certain release came from that. The Native stared at Jerod, his face and posture unmoving. The room fell silent and Bill, noting the time, closed the meeting with the Lord's Prayer. They all stood, stepping back from their chairs and held hands while they prayed. Jerod felt Bill's eyes on him the entire time.

***

There was a brusque clamor as chairs were folded and piled back against the walls. The men chatted, louder and more openly friendly, as they collected the used coffee cups and filled ash trays. A few had been assigned to the chore of cleaning up the kitchen area, and there was a hurried race for the last few cups of coffee before the pot was washed.

Eventually, a few at a time wandered out of the smoke-laden room, through the opened doors, to suck deeply at the early evening air.

"Hell, we'll all die of lung cancer instead of alcoholism!" An old man said, clapping Jerod on the back. Jerod smiled and agreed. He walked outside and saw Bill waiting for him.

"Do you have a few minutes?" Bill asked.

"Yeah, actually, I've got more than that. Is there some place around here where we can get a cup of coffee?" Jerod was clearly fascinated with this man of contradictions. He could see now that this Native man was educated, but there was nothing condescending in his manner.

They decided to take Bill's truck, an old Ford pickup that resembled something just off the Reservation more than the man, himself. There was a coffee shop about a quarter mile down the road that kept all-night hours, and the two men found an out-of-the-way table and ordered coffee. Jerod thought about the replacements that alcoholics looked for in their lives. It was rare to find a non-smoking alcoholic, or one who didn't drink coffee. Well, at least he never found any. They all had their stimulants and addictions. They were just reduced to something less devastating. Or he hoped so, as he thought of the old man's remark.

Bill did not use small talk. He introduced himself by his full name, Bill Martinez, and explained that he was both Apache and Mexican. He was direct and yet extremely courteous in his questions.

Jerod was soon telling this complete stranger about his tour of duty in Vietnam. A smile and an acknowledgment here or there put him at ease. Jerod talked at great lengths about his ambitions, Linda, and more. The thing was ... Bill did not seem like a stranger. As different as their cultural backgrounds were, there was an immediate affinity.

The Native told him that he had been in construction, but more surprisingly he told Jerod he was a medicine man in his Apache tribe. Jerod tried to imagine what this involved, and reading the questions on his face, Bill answered directly.

"I help find the source of illness in my people and by working with the Creator, and through the sick person, hope to find the cure."

Jerod was sure there was much more to it than that, and almost in anticipation Bill said, "It is more involved, but that is the essence."

Even though the itching was not as bad as it had been, Jerod absentmindedly scratched the red welts on his arms.

"How long have you had the rash?" Bill asked.

"It started yesterday. I kind of figured it had something to do with the alcohol. Maybe I'm finally allergic to it." He coughed a small laugh. "Actually, it would be the final justice."

"Why don't you tell me about the hallucination, the whole story?"

Jerod proceeded to give him the whole story. Starting with finding the bone or fossil, whatever it was, Jerod told Bill everything that happened in the last two days. When he came to the part where the masked rock spoke, he did not feel embarrassed as he had earlier. There was a difference between relating this to Bill and telling his story at an AA meeting.

Bill gently asked him to repeat the words, and Jerod recalled, "I call on you, Great Spirit. Intervene!" Bill became quiet for several minutes. The waitress came around to refill their cups once more and when she left, Bill leaned forward intently, his bronzed arms resting on the table.

He asked Jerod, "How did you feel when you heard those words?"

Jerod knew that he did not mean his initial panic, and he thought about it before he answered.

"I guess I felt like I had witnessed a prayer ... a strong prayer."

It was late when they decided to leave, and Jerod was hesitant. He felt a peculiar loss in their parting, and asked if there was some way he could get in touch with Bill. They both exchanged phone numbers and addresses, and this helped to reassure Jerod.

Bill turned thoughtful a moment and asked, "Would you allow me to see your rocks and bones?"

Jerod promised to come to next Friday's meeting and to bring the bundle with him.

***

The sun had gone down hours ago and the brilliant lights of the highway struck Jerod as artificial. Wherever he had been the last several hours, it had nothing to do with civilization. Jerod stopped at a drugstore on the way back and bought a bottle of calamine lotion.

His whole outlook was improved. He would deal with this annoying symptom, and not make everything else into a big deal. Of course, he'd promised Linda that he would see a doctor, but he didn't see how a doctor could help him at this point. If the alcohol had caused the rash and the hallucination, it would go away, because he was not going to drink again, period. Besides, he thought the rash was already fading and the lotion would cinch it.

It was nine-fifteen when he drove in to Jenny's and Pete's driveway. Their Blazer was gone and in its place was Linda's blue Camaro. Jerod entered through the kitchen door and called out her name. The house was dark, except for the pulsating blue glow of the television set in the living room.

"I'm in here, honey!"

He found her sitting on the floor in front of the TV. His crumpled shirt was spread out on the floor and Linda was apparently examining his rocks and bone. Linda's blonde hair and sun-tanned body glowed in response to the only source of light in the room. She had on shorts and a midriff top and she looked ravishing.

Suddenly the whole series of events that Jerod had been through in the last forty-eight hours seemed ridiculous. He was back. The very real sudden presence of Linda brought a sharp yearning in his groin.

"Hey, baby, what are you doing here?" But he was smiling and it was obvious to Linda that it only mattered that she was here.

He took her in his arms and crushed her pelvis into his, and now what had begun in playful yearning, became demand. Jerod touched her silky smooth hair, trailing his fingers over her cheekbone, and lifted her face to meet his mouth. He couldn't have helped himself it he had wanted to. Jerod dropped to his knees in front of her and finding her naked stomach, began to explore it carefully with his tongue. Linda undid the zipper of her shorts. Their own heat had become surprisingly violent, and Jerod took her there on the white rug, before the mindless god of television. Still on his knees, he lifted her torso and brought her home. Her golden curves began to undulate and her back arched up, rippling in the blue rays. Her blonde hair fell back, swinging free from her horizontal, throbbing body, and Jerod felt his own thrust move on and upward toward its victory.

Exhausted, they both fell to the rug, and there in rolling perspiration Jerod rocked her gently. When his own pulse, which had filled his ears with pounding, became more regular, he listened for other sounds. There was only the TV's drone and Linda's irregular breathing. From the floor, Jerod thought the rocks and bones strewn across the rug in blue iridescent light resembled an eerie moonscape.

"How are you?" Linda whispered huskily, her face just inches from his.

"I hope as good as you are," Jerod muttered, contentedly.

***

They lingered awhile on the downside of passion until finally hunger for food replaced that for each other. When they had recovered and Linda had made each of them a fried egg and onion sandwich with hot sauce just as Jerod liked it, she did not let him get by with that cute, but evasive answer. She sat back down on the floor beside him, where the television continued glowing like some oblivious idiot, and handed him his plate.

"Now, tell me. How are you?"

This time, for the third time - he couldn't help but count, he told the story of his drinking, the rocks, bone, and hallucination. Only he made such lightness of the whole thing that Linda tilted her head and gave him her cynical, disbelieving look.

"Don't look at me like some loan officer, Lady!" Jerod mockingly scolded her, tickling her ribs and sending her into spasms of laughter.

When she began choking on her sandwich, he figured he'd better stop. They spent an hour or so, on the floor catching up on their life apart. Linda told him of the note Peter and Jenny had left. They had planned on fossil hunting this weekend, and Jerod recalled that he had been told.

"There was something else in the note. Peter said to take care of the fossil, and that he would talk to you about it when he got back."

The soundness of their relationship had been reaffirmed and from this vantage point they discussed the present and future with confidence. Finally, Jerod took her hand and led her to the bedroom to confirm it just one more time before they fell asleep.

***

Chapter 6

SLOUCH

SLOUCH

The winds were unusual for this time of year. Or, at least that is what Jack Owens said. Dan had left for work at the usual time, six-forty-five, and when he stepped outside on to the porch, the wind was already blowing warm. There had only been a few hours in the early morning when the absence of the wind permitted sleep.

Dan still felt tired as he drove up to Jack's house in the Castle Hills sub-division. He tapped the horn with the engine still running and leaned groggily on the steering wheel to wait. He saw Jack exit the front door and heard Lisa exchange angry words with him.

He knew that Jack was embarrassed when he opened the door on the passenger side and only mumbled "Hi". They rode along in silence and were almost to the plant before Jack had anything more to say. Dan was content listening to the radio, mulling over a weekend project for Mandy's playhouse, and didn't feel the desire to pry into Jack's affairs.

It surprised him when Jack asked, "How do you and Ryann make it on your pay, Dan?"

"Well, it's not easy, that's for sure," Dan answered with a chuckle. When Jack failed to see the humor, Dan glanced at his passenger's face and read the seriousness in its lines.

Jack complained, "All we do is argue about money. There is never enough, even when I work overtime. So how do you do it with one income?"

"Ryann and I have talked about her going back to work, but we're both ..." A car cut in front of the Escort and Dan hit the horn, a defensive reaction rather than one of anger. When the driver threw his arm out the window and flung him the "bird", Dan wondered about his own patience.

"Anyway, we know there are other things we'll have to give up if Ryann returns to work now." Dan considered the rat race that everyone seemed part of these days, he and Ryann to a lesser degree. Maybe a very important degree, he thought, as he remembered different driving habits.

"You know, Jack, it seems we're all living on the ragged edge. And yet when I get home there is my sanity. It sounds chauvinistic, but Ryann and Mandy are there, have been there during the day. It's not just a house, it's a home because of that. I guess, I'd just as soon do without a lot, rather than give that up."

Dan thought about how this sounded, just as awkward as when he had tried in on Ryann, he was sure. Mercifully, Ryann knew him better than Jack. She knew that he wasn't trying to put one over on her, that deep inside Dan was expressing his appreciation of her as a wife and mother, and that he just wasn't very good with words.

A quick review of Jack's face told Dan he had missed his mark. There was almost a visual dismissal, a clearing of imagined webs, as Jack found his place back in his rut. There was no way Jack could accept a life with less, because he couldn't accept the idea of Dan having more. To acknowledge that would mean facing defeat. He knew of only one way to gauge more and the barometer was a financial one.

"Well, I'm going to check out a home equity loan in Phoenix. The banks around here are pretty tight, but I hear Grand West is making loans." Jack's face became more relaxed as he talked, and Dan saw that it came from being on familiar ground.

With Jack's problem back in Jack's apparent control, Dan took the Wilson exit and followed a line of traffic to the plant's huge parking lot. He still hadn't come to terms with this massive, fenced, security-monitored parking lot in the middle of the desert. Just like the tracts of new homes, the aircraft plant formed its own kind of desert -- a bleak entity without soul and therefore, of course, without character.

Even so, once through the careful security check: cleared, processed, and finally turned over to his department, Dan enjoyed the challenges of his job. Walking the huge, gray, echoing corridors it was easy to feel displaced, but as Dan turned the corner and read his own name among the others on the door he found his oasis in the desert.

It was here in this gray area that he was to set black apart from white, making it his responsibility, with other engineers, to set the standards for the quality the United States government demanded, yet had no means to achieve on its own. Key parts for the boosters that would thrust the next satellite into space were in the hands of individual men. For that reason, Dan still had hope. He knew his own ambitions, his own caring for perfection, and so he believed in himself. It was a small leap of faith to believe in America's space program and considerable satisfaction to know that he was part of it.

Dan would have felt smug, but it wasn't in his character. He'd work a full day at a job that he really enjoyed, and then he'd go home to a weekend with those he loved. His life was very good, and he felt it only human nature that at the apex of such contemplation a shadow would cross his thoughts. There was no other way to describe this ghost of a feeling that flowed through his mind, leaving him with a lingering chill on this hot, blowing Monday in early June.

***

It was time to make Slouch legal. They had four months of Arizona under their belts and still hadn't licensed the dog. Besides, this wiry canine had a pesky cough that Ryann was determined to have checked. She remembered hearing somewhere that a cough could be linked to a worm infestation. And to think he slept with Mandy!

Ryann had remembered the veterinarian hospital close to the school and had called to make an appointment to take him there this morning. The receptionist had said that wouldn't be necessary, just to bring him on in.

"Well, dog, let's do it!" Ryann said, making vocal the final commitment.

Slouch looked skeptically at the leash. They would be walking several blocks to the vet's and this was the way it was going to be, Ryann thought. The second car would only come when there was a second income. Another argument in support of her looking for work, and then she reminded herself of that ever-revolving door; she would need a car to get to work and a job to afford a car.

Slouch crouched down, his ears plastered to the sides of his head, as Ryann clipped the leash to his collar. All of the dog's usual confidence departed the moment he saw a restraint on his freedom. He fixed Ryann with an eye-level stare and whined his disapproval. Ryann couldn't help but remember the many times that Dan had stopped the car to walk Slouch on their trip west. They hadn't made it all the way out here to have Slouch plastered over Devonshire Avenue. Just the thought of explaining to Mandy that her dog had gone to doggie heaven was enough to make Ryann nauseous.

But it was only luck that they hadn't lost him. The three-foot, redwood fence that enclosed the back yard had been built for the previous owner's cocker spaniel. It became a wonderful game for Slouch, as his long Airedale legs carried him back and forth at will. Because he was not a vicious dog, Ryann had to laugh at the thought of this lanky, frazzle-haired canine baring his teeth. They hadn't worried about him biting the mailman. Their concern had been that he might follow him home.

The screen door slammed behind Ryann, as Slouch lunged at the leash with a sudden new attitude. He'd accepted his assignment to explore the neighborhood, and was just barely tolerant of taking Ryann along for the ride.

"Whoa!" Ryann yelled, and she grasped a tighter rein on the leash. She could be as stubborn as he was unmanageable, Ryann assured herself. After some stumbling down the porch steps, she dug in her heels and settled Slouch into an awkward gambol.

They had bumbled along Devonshire, Ryann with her eyes fixed on the sidewalk ahead of her and Slouch darting from one side to the other sniffing history, when they came to the corner of Devonshire and Vine. This was the busy intersection that ran in front of Mandy's elementary school. Fortunately, Slouch had never roamed this far before. Ryann was certain they would have lost him to the status of school mascot if he had. School was in session and there were no kids on the playground, and there were no crossing guards on the corner, either.

Reminding herself of the danger she had instilled in Mandy, she stepped into the street with Slouch drawn up close to her pant legs. Ryann was just priding herself on a tight ship when a yellow El Camino came out of nowhere, radio booming, and presumably truant teenagers yelling at the top of their lungs. The car sent Ryann two-stepping back to the curb, and in that moment when she was looking to save her own life, her hand lost its grip. The next thing she saw was Slouch running up Vine, yelping in fear.

Her heart pounded at the sickening reality that Slouch was not her dog. She could call to him all the way to Phoenix and he would pay no attention. Mandy, on the other hand, had just to pout and the Airedale was at her side, whimpering in sympathy. Though it seemed a lost cause from the beginning, there was no way Ryann could accept his loss.

Ryann took off after the dog, her hip pack flapping at her waist. Even in her dash to catch Slouch, she was thankful that she was wearing jeans, not carrying a bag, and that her hands were free. It was bad enough that she could imagine what she looked like as she streaked by the windows of houses. Even in the heat of her sprint, she saw herself as no ordinary jogger. She ran hell-bent-for-leather and still the distance between her and Slouch lengthened. The trailing leash was no longer visible, and soon she even lost sight of the dog.

***

Slouch had forgotten the chase, and the car that had come bearing down on them. This was an adventure. An occasional dog would bark its warning from one of the yards he passed, but there was always the next yard and new smells. He wandered up the block, crisscrossing lawns, relieving himself on this tree and that shrub, but never seeing a human along the way. He was limping now and his rear right leg stiffly accommodated his gait, like a misfit part brought along to prop him up.

When Slouch came to the vacant lot and construction site, the newly turned earth smells absorbed his attention. He followed his nose, that had actually turned pink from rubbing the ground, and in his preoccupation almost ran into the man.

"Hey, guy, what are you doing here?" Jerod saw the lead the dog was dragging behind him. It was obvious that this was a recent escapee.

"Wouldn't you know it, he came to find his bone," called Rick from the seat of the back hoe.

Jerod ignored this reference to his own recent occupation.

"Come here, boy!"

Slouch didn't need an invitation. His tail was wagging the rest of his scrawny body. He was panting and drooling with excitement, and when he saw Jerod pour some water from the construction crew's community thermos into a hard hat he whined in eager expectation. The dog lapped greedily, slopping streams of water in every direction.

Jerod patted the dog's wiry head and smiled. It was his first diversion since coming back to the job, and he found his shoulders loosening up. He really hadn't worked out a plan for this morning. There was still the unsettled matter of the fossils. Ethically and he supposed legally, the excavation had to come to a halt until it could be determined what was at stake.

He was avoiding the issue without jeopardizing the "dig," he told himself. Rick and Bill were working at the other end of the lot, and it really wouldn't matter if he poked around with just hand tools, except for the fact that the rash was driving him crazy.

The bottle of calamine lotion he bought on Friday was in the truck. With luck there was enough to quiet the itch until he could get to the convenience store at noon. When the dog followed him to the truck, Jerod noticed the stiff leg.

"You're not in very good shape either, are you?"

Jerod looked up to see a woman running toward them yelling, "Grab his leash!"

He felt rather foolish, but obediently picked up the end of the leash. The dog made no effort to run. The dog looked curiously from Jerod to Ryann, as if to determine what was next.

It was obvious the young woman was the caboose in this chase. Her face was flushed and a mass of untamed auburn curls flew about her shoulders.

"Oh, I'm sorry! I didn't mean to bark directions," Ryann blushed as she realized her unintentional pun. "It's just that he's a handful and I don't want him to get away again."

"That's all right, but I don't think he's going anywhere."

Ryann looked down at the man's loose hold on Slouch's leash, and noticed that in his other hand he was holding a large bottle of calamine lotion.

Slouch began his hacking cough, and Jerod suggested that he give him another drink.

"Thanks. I really do appreciate your catching him. I'm on my way to the vet with Slouch ... that's his name. Hopefully, they'll find out what's causing the cough." Ryann found she was a little embarrassed at the condition of her dog. She could see he was limping, too, as they walked over to the hard hat filled with water.

Reading her thoughts, Jerod said, "We make a pair, your dog and me. I was just going to put some of this stuff on my hands. If you'll excuse me, this itch is driving me wild."

Ryann watched as the construction worker, evidently possessed with an itch, poured some of the white liquid into the palm of his hand and spread it on his forearms and the back of his hands. He sighed in obvious relief.

"Maybe its kennel cough," Jerod speculated. "I don't know what mine is. Should I see your vet?"

Ryann suspected his eyes held a humor not often shown to others. She knew she was one of the privileged. There was something contradictory in the way his face broke into a smile, like there had been a long absence between happy times. Suddenly he stuck out his hand, but then immediately retracted it to his side.

"My turn to be sorry! I didn't introduce myself, but on second thought, you'd better not shake my hand. I really don't know what this creeping crud is and I wouldn't want to give it to you. Jerod Axsom of Axsom Excavation, at your service," he ended with a flourish.

"Ryann Thearle, dog catcher. And this is my daughter's dog, Slouch."

The two of them laughed while Slouch continued to explore the hole in the ground.

"Would you mind if I had a drink? It's getting hot!"

Jerod found a clean paper cup and poured her a drink from the big thermos. Ryann relaxed. Her fast-paced jog to catch Slouch must have earned her a few extra minutes.

A growl came from the cool shadows of the hole and Ryann instinctively looked for Slouch. It took her a moment to realize that it was, indeed, her dog. Slouch's growl was low and drawn with suspicion. When Ryann and Jerod went over to the edge of the pit to inquire, the dog began barking in earnest. Soon, he was yelping and backing from the earthen wall where Jerod had been digging.

The dog was frantic now and fixed his eyes on the site until the last possible moment, visually pinning down the enemy,

Ryann mused. Then he quickly turned and scrambled up the bank with his tail between his legs. Slouch ran straight to Jerod and flattened his quivering body against the man's leg, as if to make his self invisible. Whatever it was, Ryann couldn't find any evidence in the hole. She had never seen Slouch so frightened and that was almost as alarming as the fact that he looked to this stranger to save him.

"I don't know what got into him," Ryann said, flustered. "But I'm certain we need to get out of your way and let you get back to work."

Jerod had crouched down with a very quiet hand on the dog's head. Slouch began to calm under its soothing presence. There seemed to be a communion between the dog and the man, and Ryann had the curious feeling that they had forgotten she was there.

"You've been very kind and ... well, I suppose we'll be late for our appointment." As soon as she said it, she considered her absurd need to rush, and worse yet, offer a lie as an excuse. She called to the dog, more to reaffirm her ownership than in hopes of his obedience. Slowly the reverie evaporated. Ryann walked over and quietly picked up the leash. Jerod blinked and smiled up at her in renewed recognition.

"I hope he'll be all right. He's a good dog, and I'll bet your little girl would be real worried if anything happened to him."

***

Once at the veterinarian's office, Slouch became more like his old self. Curiously, he tried to snoop and sniff, and cough at the few pets in the waiting room. In contrast, in a corner of the room a large Mastiff sat trembling next to his owner, whimpering at the hospital smells.

When it was their turn to see the vet, Slouch limped into the examination room ready to continue his adventure. Dr. Chase, a kind, elderly gentleman, managed to examine Slouch anyway. He asked Ryann questions about his eating habits, the cough, and the limp. The veterinarian, apparently the senior in this partnership, spoke assuredly and said he thought an X-ray was in order. Ryann was directed back out front to wait for the results.

The large Mastiff was called in, plus a Beagle, two cats, and a tortoise, before Ryann was told the doctor would see her again.

"It's as I suspected," Dr. Chase said brightly. "Slouch, here, has a case of Coccidioidomycosis. Have you heard of Valley Fever?" he asked. "It's the same thing, and called San Joaquin Valley Fever, too."

Ryann hadn't, of course, and listened as Dr. Chase explained that it was caused by a fungus found in their desert region. The X-ray had shown the fuzzy areas on the lungs. Slouch's symptom was classic -- a persistent cough. Even the limp, only discovered today, was part of the arthritic attack of the disease on joints.

Yes, it could be cured and they would begin a course of antibiotics, administered over a couple of weeks. And that was really all that Ryann wanted to hear.

***

Ryann realized that it was past lunch-time when she walked pass the front of the construction site and saw that Jerod Axsom's truck was gone. The other workers were there and she waved to them, but she kept a tight grip on Slouch's leash. She did not want to go through the pit-and-the-pendulum experience again.

She couldn't help but think about the story she had to tell Dan when he got home from work. "Guess what happened to me on the way to the vet," she recited to herself.

***

Chapter 7

DIAGNOSIS

DIAGNOSIS

Ryann barely entered the door, or so it seemed, when Mandy came home from school. The thought of school children on foot merging with Slouch's and her lane of traffic made her think that the day could have been more exciting after all. She kicked off her tennis shoes and found the cool, bare floor soothing. Who would have thought tennis shoes could hurt your feet?

"Is Slouch going to be all right?" Mandy asked earnestly.

"Yes. We just have to make sure we remember to give him his medicine. You can help with that. Do you want some Kool Aid, Mandy?"

Mandy was sitting cross-legged in front of her dog. She cooed sympathetic little sounds that seemed to convince Slouch that he was dying. He bent his head, questioning and whined his reply.

Ryann still felt the dog's fear back at the construction site. It had made a haunting impression on her and she found that for the first time she was reaching to understand the dog's psyche. Slouch had always been "the dog", or Mandy's property. Ryann, herself, had regarded him as something to be tolerated. Not that she would have ever mistreated him. She believed in the humane treatment of all animals, but anything beyond physical care had not come from her.

Mandy, on the other hand, had real empathy for her dog. Ryann had at least recognized it and knew that it was something she wanted to nurture in her daughter. She wasn't sure that it was a virtue or a sixth sense, but it was somehow a part of an evolution of the spirit. For the first time, Ryann found she wanted to learn more about it, even nurture it in herself, as well.

She sat on the floor beside Mandy and Slouch, with two glasses of Kool Aid, and they pretended the swamp cooler over their heads was doing its job. Down at this level, reduced by size, Ryann became the invisible one. Mandy chatted with her dog, communicating her wisdom.

"Don't you worry, Slouch, my friend will help you. He knows the way."

Mandy spoke in a whisper and her voice was almost inaudible, but Ryann didn't question her further. She didn't want to break the spell and she sensed that Slouch somehow understood every word.

***

Later, when Dan returned from work, Ryann told him what the vet had said. She'd forgotten the medical term, but conveyed the general diagnosis and prescribed care. She admitted to Dan that she was actually relieved that it wasn't worms, or something contagious. Her imagined fears, of God-knows-what infecting Mandy as she slept, could have made it an issue between her and Dan.

When it was Mandy's bedtime and she had crawled under the lone sheet wearing just a worn cotton slip because of the heat, Dan sat on the edge of her bed and told her about his plan for their weekend.

"You can help me build the playhouse, Mandy. We're going to use some palm branches for the roof just like we saw at the desert park, remember?"

But she was already asleep. Dan was certain she was faking. Her head had just hit the pillow, but her breathing had already found its slow, even pattern and her eyelashes lay still, just barely touching those tender cheeks. Another big day, he supposed. He turned off the light by the bed, and left Slouch lying on the braided rug to guard his pal.

***

In his own bed, Ryann waited in serious thought. Dan guessed her concerns were for Mandy and her sick dog. It came as a surprise when she said, "Mandy did it again. You know ... her strange comments out of nowhere."

Dan was struggling to take off his boots, and he looked up sharply. He knew, without asking, what Ryann was talking about. Not this particular time maybe, but the unexplained statements had come just frequently enough to haunt him, too. In fact, wasn't he trying just the other day to recall others?

He listened while Ryann related the latest. When she finished, Dan realized that he in fact didn't have anything to add. This fell in the category of UFO's. He couldn't reinforce that of which he had no evidence, but he couldn't deny the words out of his daughter's mouth either.

When Ryann didn't continue, he thought she felt the same way. Dan turned out the light, and reached under the sheets to pull her gently toward him, spoon fashion.

***

Sometime in the night Dan heard a muffled noise and immediately sought in the dark for the only light, the red numerals of the digital clock. Five forty-eight. What woke him at this hour? Dan stopped his own breathing and listened intently. There it was, again, Mandy's cry. Probably a nightmare, he thought. He left the bed as quietly as possible. No use waking Ryann, he reasoned. This was one of the rare times that she hadn't jumped responding to Mandy's call for a drink of water.

Dan padded into Mandy's bedroom. She was crying, all right. "What's the matter kid? Did you have a bad dream?" Dan clicked on the light and stared at his daughter.

The child looked ridiculously, yet menacingly, comical. Red blotches covered her face and neck, and stood out as a raw blaze in contrast with her fair hair and the white sheet. The bedding covered the rest of her body, but he was pretty sure whatever this was didn't stop at her neck.

"I don't feel good, Daddy!" she cried.

She didn't look good. Dan's first thought was which childhood disease this could be. His second thought, which embarrassed him the moment it flashed its ugly warning, was his own personal history of remembered childhood diseases. Dan put a fatherly handle on his rising panic and went to her side. He placed his hand gingerly on her forehead. She was hot.

"What's the matter?" Ryann was standing in the doorway, fully awake now that she saw Mandy's face.

Dan went to get a glass of water and the thermometer, while Ryann checked her over. When he came back in the room Mandy was leaning over the bed heaving violently into a trashcan Ryann had hurriedly placed there. The skin that seemed to float around her red welts looked milky white and eerily pale in comparison. He could see that her torso looked wicked, now that Ryann had removed her slip.

"Chicken pox would look more like little isolated blisters, and she had measles when she was four, but there is more than one kind and I can't remember anything about them."

Dan could hear the attempt at control in Ryann's voice as it wound around in a tighter spiral seeking a logical explanation. He tried to offer some assistance.

"What about scarlet fever? I mean this is red!" His emphasis weakened as he thought about what effect this observation might have on his daughter.

With Mandy's weak little body plopped back against the pillow, Ryann tenderly wiped her mouth with a Kleenex and asked if she wanted a drink of water.

"But maybe we'd better take your temperature first, huh, baby?" She remembered almost too late.

Both parents sat on either side of their daughter's bed and counted the one-thousand-and, two-thousand-and until they marked the two minutes needed to read the thermometer.

"Jeez, 104," Ryann said, half under her breath. "I'm calling the doctor."

***

Mandy felt every bit as sick as the time her dad had taken her on the scary ride at the fair. She just wished everything would stand still, that her stomach would be still, that people would just leave her alone, and let her sleep. But they didn't.

Her parents bundled up Mandy and Dan carried her to the car. Dan laid her on the back seat with a pillow for her head. The bowl they placed beside her was just a reminder that she would probably be sick again. Mandy found that even though she tried to not think about it, she imagined those things certain to turn her stomach, like pork chops ... oh, yuck. She could smell them, and though she tried to will away the smell she had no power to do so.

In the early morning light they made the trip to the doctor's office. Mandy kept her eyes open and watched the telephone poles and wires fly by the car window. It was a sickening illusion, like the video film her dad had first taken, before he learned to control the camera. When Mandy cried, Ryann suggested she close her eyes, but she found this made her dizzier

***

Mandy moaned and whimpered, much like the dog, Ryann thought, and for the first time she remembered the sick dog. Slouch had avoided their path as she and Dan had hurried about getting Mandy ready. She couldn't even remember seeing him until they were ready to leave. Then she had noticed Slouch was in his place of vigil, the braided rug by Mandy's bed, and no amount of coaxing or orders would make him budge. Well, at least he wouldn't be jumping the fence, Ryann assured herself.

Suddenly Ryann saw yesterday's adventure in a new perspective: Slouch, the construction site, Jerod Axsom and his rash. Yes, he had a rash, too. Obviously, Mandy didn't get it from him, but it was most likely the same contagious disease. When she found out what it was, she must remember to let Jerod Axsom know the cause of his itching. She supposed the close proximity to the school was how he caught it, whatever "it" was.

***

The receptionist at the clinic had said to bring Mandy in the door on the side of the building. All possibly contagious diseases entered here. They appeared like fugitives from society, Mandy in Dan's arms and Ryann bringing up the trailing blanket, trying to look as inconspicuous as possible as they passed other early morning patients in the parking lot. It was Tuesday and Dan felt it fortunate that the clinic was open; it was closed on Wednesdays and Sundays, the sign on the door read.

Dan was assigned his odd-parent-out seat in the waiting room, while Ryann braved the darker corridors of the examining rooms. Dan tried to dismiss his irrational fear. He was a grown man, for God's sake, and today's medical knowledge had already saved Ryann's life. That was a fact. So log one for reason, he told himself. But behind this logical part of his brain, recessed in some primeval corner, was the deeper suspicion that doctors had nothing to do with life and death. They might make the time we had here more comfortable with their morphine and placebos, but an issue as great as mortality was in the providence of God. And that was not necessarily reassuring.

The Thearle family had, Dan thought, a customary relationship with God ... religion by design. He laughed unconsciously, and the matronly receptionist looked out curiously from the window of her cubicle. Dan politely covered his mouth and feigned a cough. Just another example of how we aim to please, he reminded himself cynically.

But wasn't it true? Shortly after they had moved to Tucson they had sought out the neighborhood church, sort of like the search and happy discovery of the convenience store in the next block. These were the necessities of civilized life; a place to sing hymns on Sunday mornings and to bring food for the poor during the holidays, and equally close in the other direction, a market to pick up a quart of milk when it was too late to drive to the supermarket. Dan suspected his relationship with God was one of equal convenience. Maybe he should propose at the next Young Christian's meeting that they rename their church the Church of Heavenly Convenience.

It wasn't that Dan doubted there was a God, he just didn't know Him very well. He supposed that one of his most secret fears was that some day he would need to know, seek to know, and find nothing. He was not one to abandon reason when he needed it most, and he was almost certain that anything beyond faithful attendance at the church of their choice would require some kind of mind betrayal. He felt unworthy when he thought about this, as he recognized his own doubting faith. His timing was all too obvious. The old atheist-in-the-foxhole believer, Dan thought.

But that really wasn't true, was it? Believing in God, and man, too, for that matter, was not the same as trusting Him. That required communication, and just like the doctors who couldn't seem to reduce their Latin to layman terms, Dan suspected his prayers went to some celestial dead-letter office, too.

These were thoughts that could drive you crazy if you let them. Dan stared at the hallway, willing Ryann and Mandy to come back.

***

It seemed like forever. Mandy laid cold and shivering, on the paper-covered examination table. Ryann had covered her, as best she could, with the blanket they had brought from home. It was chilly in here, though Ryann was certain that outside the day was warming. Ryann felt the chill of helplessness, too, but she wouldn't allow this a toehold. Motherhood demanded more.

Finally, the door handle turned and a young doctor greeted them with a friendly smile. Dr. Harrison brought with him his welcomed personal warmth. Ryann thought their banished room of quarantine wasn't quite so cold.

The doctor checked Mandy carefully, and said that he thought this looked like a classic case of Valley Fever. He did not feel that immediate antibiotic treatment was necessary, unless several tests proved this to be more than a primary coccidioidal infection. Ryann listened as he explained that usually all that was needed was restriction of activity and treatment for the symptoms, such as calamine lotion for the rash.

Ryann felt immediate relief, but now Slouch became the enemy, as she thought about his infection. She told the doctor about the dog's diagnosis, and he reassured her that the disease, though highly infectious, was not contagious. The dog and Mandy shared a mutual environment and this was the only connection. That would probably be the diagnosis for the fellow at the construction site, too, Ryann thought. When she asked Dr. Harrison about this possibility, he said it was a common disease for those working in the Arizona soil.

"It's a hazard of the trade, and for other professions, as well. Archaeologists working here or in California or even Mexico, run a high risk. It can be more dangerous for some people, particularly dark-skinned adults, but in many cases the patient never knows he's been exposed. Mandy's going to be fine, I'm sure."

Again, Ryann found herself sent back to a waiting room, while an X-ray was ordered for Mandy. Looking across the small cubicle that was the infectious disease waiting area, Ryann saw an expression of terrible isolation on Dan's face. He was battling it out alone, the last to know, and in the meanwhile left with his imagination. She was sure that it was running wild.

"Honey, she'll be fine." Ryann found herself repeating the doctor's exact words, the ones she had wanted to hear. The ones Dan would want to hear.

"Dr. Harrison thinks its Valley Fever and he is doing a couple of tests to confirm it. Mandy is getting an X-ray right now."

Ryann could see the premature conclusions begin to form as worry lines, and headed off the brewing storm. "No, it's not the dog that gave it to her. I thought the same thing, but apparently it's found in the ground around here."

Dan took her hand and squeezed it hard. He grinned broadly, and his blue eyes squinted back the shallow pool that threatened to cloud his vision. He was dearer to her in that moment than any Ryann could remember, and she found her own eyes grow moist. She was glad that they were alone in the waiting room, as she put her arms around Dan's shoulders and pulled him to her breast. They hugged, protectively encircling their love.

***

Dan thought professionals have such a way of putting things back in perspective. The heavier questions that had earlier eaten at his soul began to fade, and he reminded himself of the similarity even in his own profession. We can't all know everything. That's why there are engineers and doctors.

He wondered how vulnerable Dr. Harrison would feel, flying in those friendly skies on a wing and a prayer; one in which he had helped design, he reminded himself. No matter the devotion to your particular skill, we are all at the mercy of the skills of others. Like ducks out of water, we're all birds of a feather, Dan chuckled.

Half the day was shot when they got home, and Dan didn't really want to go in to work. It was hardly worth the travel time, and besides he had called the plant earlier. No one expected him in today. His own job loyalty served him well, now that he needed time off. Even Jack Owens had said so.

"Fuck the job, Dan. When's the last time you took a day off? Besides, I was going to call you. I'm not going to be in today, either. Think I'll drive over to Phoenix and pay a visit to that bank I told you about."

It had been a good decision to stay home. They had stopped at the drug store to pick up Junior Strength Tylenol and calamine lotion, and though Dan couldn't think of another errand right now, there was at least the Escort if Ryann needed to make a trip.

The house was already hot despite their closing the drapes earlier to shut out the sun. Mandy's room was hotter yet, having reflected the eastern sun all morning. Dan wanted to put her on the couch, but she weakly protested and whispered that she wanted her own bed.

He carried Mandy into her bedroom, feeling the heat emanate from her little body. Amazingly, he watched her shiver with chills. Maybe this room was better after all. Dan placed her gently on the unmade bed, and looked around appreciatively at all of her things. Like sentries, toys and stuffed animals gazed down from the shelves that Dan had built. A bear rested lazily against several books, the biggest a copy of Grimm's Fairy Tales, stories from which Dan had been reading to Mandy. In the corner, was the small red table and two chairs that he and Ryann had bought in Nogales, Mexico. A design of small yellow and white flowers danced on slender green vines, giving a whimsical nature to the miniature furniture. In each chair sat another stuffed bear, hunched in mock ferocity over a tiny china tea cup. The room was sweetly reassuring in its perpetual moment of captured youth.

Slouch was lying on the rug, where Ryann remembered seeing him last, and looked up appreciatively at their return. Ryann fussed around Mandy's bed, fluffing her pillow and covering her with the sheet and the thinnest of several blankets. Tenderly, she coated Mandy's rash with calamine lotion, and then remembered there was another patient. The dog was overdue for his morning pill. This was going to be fun, she thought, a regular infirmary.

Mandy was already asleep, and Dan and Ryann left the room quietly. Dan called to the dog once. Slouch only lifted an ear, but still refused to budge.

***

Chapter 8

SOMETHING MORE

SOMETHING MORE

The bright sun rose quickly in the sky. Just a moment ago it lay hidden behind the cardboard mountains that added their own rugged gray-blue layers to the horizon. Even at this early hour Linda could feel the heat of El Sol boring a path across the Phoenix desert. The miracle was that there was still coolness in the air, a remnant of the night before. The contrast was vibrant and Linda felt herself being recharged. There was something about life on the desert, and regardless of how Phoenix had grown vertically, in Linda's mind it would always be a desert that made her feel closer to the rest of the solar system. The power was always there. The sun would become everything as it burned and etched its dominion over humanity.

It was during these few minutes, driving to work, that Linda drew on the sun's strength like a jump start from a battery. She knew she was one of the fortunate who could escape behind the heavy double doors of the bank. There she could lock herself into a cooler world. Jerod wasn't so lucky.

When Jerod called Monday afternoon he had been tired, exhausted really, but happy enough. Arizona summers could be extremely cruel to those who worked outdoors, but he adjusted fairly well. In any case, he seemed excited about a book that he had begun and a little apologetic about wanting to get back to it. She, herself, felt rested and she checked the Tuesday sheet of her appointment calendar to see what was scheduled. A Mr. Jack Owens would be in at ten o'clock to apply for a home-equity loan.

***

As it turned out, Pete and Jenny did not return Sunday night. Jerod had reluctantly put Linda on the road about seven o'clock. He was concerned for her safety and had managed to convince her she needed a good night's sleep, which she wasn't about to have lying in bed next to him. They had prepared dinner, an elaborate affair that had required the use of almost every pot and pan in the Caulfield kitchen. It had been worth it when Jerod carried the platter, heaped with roast leg of lamb and steaming, parsley new potatoes, to the dining room where Linda gaily applauded his entrance. But after their grand time playing king and queen, when Jerod was alone to face the dishes, he began to wonder what had happened to Linda's brother and his wife.

It had been a great weekend, one that had begun so terrifyingly, way back last Friday. Jerod found it hard to believe that it had really happened, the hallucination, and even the trip to AA and the meeting with Bill Martinez all seemed like a surrealistic dream. Linda had come, and with her had come daylight. The rash was still present, and he had a headache and sore throat, but his head was on straight. No more strange trips into the Twilight Zone.

Jerod was just putting away the last of the dishes when the phone rang. The connection crackled a little, but it was clearly Pete's voice.

"We're having some luck here, Jerod. I think you can count us out tonight. Jenny and I checked into this little motel, and want to get an early start back at the dig tomorrow." Pete sounded exhilarated and a little out of breath. Jerod thought that it might have been the other way around if Pete had called, say last night.

"Actually, I thought I'd better give you a ring and let you know not to worry about us. We're up here in the Four Corners and we may stay several more days." And now his voice lowered, becoming more confidential.

"That is, if you don't think you'll be needing us ..." Pete paused, waiting for Jerod to fill in the blanks.

"No, no. I'm fine," Jerod assured him. "You go ahead. Linda's been down for the weekend and we've had a great time."

This did more to quiet any concern that Pete might have had than anything Jerod could have said. He knew his sister and her stable influence on Jerod.

"Oh, one thing, I forgot about the fossil. I think you have part of an Arctotherium mandible there. Quite a rare find, bear fossils of the Pleistocene era. Most of the Megafauna were carried off in erosion. Anyway, its speculation, but we'll check on it further when I come back. You do know to protect the site, don't you?"

And that was the rub, the one thing with which he had not dealt. Jerod wasn't sure why he had just let the problem free-float, except that in some way it was *his* site and that just didn't quite fit in with calling the developer. He could imagine the reaction of Hugh Larson of Larson and Associates. First would be his fury. After all, the job was running considerably behind schedule as it was.

"... and I think we both would agree that the delays have been mostly your responsibility." It would be like Hugh to immediately take the offensive. "Do you have any idea what kind of expenditure this company is putting out for each day added till completion?"

Jerod had a pretty good idea. He was working by the job, and there wouldn't be any take-home pay until it was completed. That fact, plus the payroll that had to be met each Friday for his two workers, meant his own bank account was all but turned inside out. At that point in the conversation any possible decisions would be out of Jerod's hands. There was only one way to maintain control and that was to protect the site himself.

"Don't worry. I'll make sure it's not disturbed." And then before Pete could ask him how he intended to guarantee this, Jerod told him not to worry about the yard. He would water it, and was there anything else Pete wanted him to do?

But Pete was quite absorbed with his own find, somewhere in the corner of the state where Arizona met its three neighbors.

"I'm sure everything will be fine, so don't send out the troops unless it's an emergency." Before Pete hung up, he gave the name and phone number of the motel where they were staying. If Jerod knew Pete, and he thought he did, the motel would be a base camp, of sorts; just a place to provide a shower every few days, and as he said, a number in case of an emergency.

Pete and Jenny all but lived out of the Blazer. There was hardly room to put the groceries in back ... when they were home long enough to go shopping ... since the tent and camp gear filled every nook and cranny. They lived and breathed "hunting," and it didn't require a gun or a camera, just time, wheels, and a pick and shovel. It was an enviable job, the more Jerod thought about it.

Monday had arrived, in spite of his daydreaming. In the back of Jerod's mind he knew there were things not faced ... rocks not turned, if you will. But he had learned two precious lessons from AA and that was, "Easy does it", and "One day at a time". He wasn't certain how these two pieces of AA wisdom applied to other alcoholics, but he had a feeling that there were many, like himself, who could get into a whole mess of trouble when they pushed or rushed. No action taken was preferable to his making un-correctable mistakes.

So he had taken the easy way out, temporarily. At the same time he indulged his curiosity, poking around in the dirt. Everything had been fine, until the dog came along and decided to do the same thing.

It struck Jerod that he might have made a mistake after all, by not taking any action. He had assumed this whole business with the rocks and fossil was behind him, but postponing a course of action was one thing, denying the need for one was quite another. The dog had brought it all home. The dog couldn't ignore it or wish it away. Slouch, that was his name, he remembered, reacted involuntarily. The hair had gone up on the back of his neck, as he had growled and whined pitifully.

Face it, three days ago the hair had stood up on Jerod's own neck, and he was sure he had done a bit of whining, too. Then he had spent the weekend playing house with Linda, rearranging reality so that it wasn't quite as terrifying as the vague memory of Friday. For one very clear moment Jerod stepped out of himself and saw the games people play, namely his own.

The dog, with his uncomplicated instincts, validated it. What it? Something, for sure, he thought. Jerod wasn't certain he really wanted to know, because that something might require that he walk on the wild side to understand.

That same "something" that made his and Linda's intuition ... or telepathy, whatever you want to call it, look like child play. He remembered how, when they were younger, he and his brother Mikey had strung two tin cans together with a string. When he pulled the string taut, he could hear his brother asking, over and over, "Can you hear me?" And yes, he could, but he had been so entranced with reinventing the telephone that he hadn't bothered to answer. That, of course, had so exasperated his big brother, that he had demanded they exchange cans to see if just maybe this was a one-way call.

Jerod felt an uneasy swelling in some part of his brain, like a primitive recollection begging to escape. As he tried to focus on this elusive thought, all the connections suddenly broke and it simply danced away like splintered sunlight. For lack of a better phrase, he again thought of the unexplainable as "something more".

After the woman and the dog left to keep their appointment with the vet, and the moment of confirmation had released its hold, Jerod looked around as if he had just awakened. The foggy state, which had permitted him to balance ... precariously, at best ... his job and his frenzied search in the dirt, receded and he faced the events of the past few days.

His very presence, standing here in the sun with sweat rolling off his neck and shoulders, was no less real than the rock that talked. By now, the earlier experience, if it were the D.T.'s, would have diminished with a healthier, more sober perspective. Instead of a startling jolt of fear, which is what he would have expected to feel fast on the heels of this admission, he felt a giddy anticipation.

Jerod looked longingly in the direction the dog had taken and wished for a chance to thank him, hug him even. The dog had brought a gift, a gift as precious as sobriety, and though he hadn't sorted it all out yet, it had something to do with sanity.

***

Jerod not only knocked off for lunch, but for the day. It had been easy enough to reroute the excavation work for Rick and Bill. Jerod had other plans. The first was to buy another bottle of calamine lotion, and the second was to get some food into his growling stomach.

He drove to the Burger Stop and bought two bacon and cheeseburgers, a large fries, and a vanilla malt. On the way home he found the aroma all too tempting. When he pulled the pickup into the Caulfield's driveway, he had but one bacon cheeseburger and the malt. He wondered how he could be sick with such an appetite. But it was undeniable that the rash was still with him. He still had a headache, too.

Once in the house Jerod dropped the remains of his lunch on the coffee table, and went to the large oak bookshelf that framed the fireplace. He had eyed some interesting books in the Caulfield collection, and had thought that one day, when he had time on his hands, he would browse through them. Now, however, he was looking for a particular cover design that had caught his attention earlier. Jerod noticed that many of the books were worse for wear. This was not a library to impress visitors, but a source of reference and information in the areas that were of interest to Pete.

There were five or six books on geology, several on mining and prospecting, a rather large volume that followed weather patterns back through recorded history, and ventured theories on the cause of ice ages of different eras. Many of the books were no longer in print, and some had ragged covers, though Jerod was certain that it wasn't as a result of Pete's abuse.

On the third shelf, almost eye-level, Jerod skimmed through titles and saw that the volumes here were primarily about Native Americans of the southwest. He supposed it made sense that Pete would be interested in Native culture, because so many times he had talked about the Native tools and artifacts that they had found.

He browsed this shelf the very day he had arrived at Jenny and Pete's. Jerod tilted his head to the right, straining to read the titles, and an idle thought entered his mind that, perhaps, librarians had a permanent list to their heads as a result of their jobs. He pulled out books randomly, selecting only the ones with their jackets intact.

There it was, a large, but slender volume titled "Tribal Dances of the Apache Tribes". On the front of its jacket were many figures dancing across the cover, colorful little animated characters dressed in tribal costumes and headdresses. Jerod turned over the book and found what he sought. Here was a large, black, masked skull or head. In comparison with the costumes on the front of the book, this fellow was plain. Only the dancer's eyes could be seen through the slits cut in what looked like a leather, close-fitting, mask. At the top of the head the mask closed tightly around a bunch of feathers. The illustration was drawn or painted accurately, not like the cover figures of whimsical cartoons, and though it was plain, it was strikingly dramatic and familiar.

This was the character who had stared back at him from the bedside table. Confronting him face to face brought back all the earlier feelings of heightened authenticity. Jerod took the book over to the sofa and opened its cover.

The book, following an introduction, was divided into sections representing the six different tribes of Apache. There were many illustrations describing the elaborate costumes, and accompanying text explaining the reasons for the dances. Jerod found that he would skim several pages, or even chapters, find an intriguing drawing, and then read for awhile. He was looking for the mask on the cover, but there was so much more. Nonetheless, he had thumbed through the sections on the Western, Chiricahua, Mescalero, Jicarilla, Lipan, and Kiowa tribes, and was just beginning again, more slowly this time, when he came upon his masked man.

It was the Chiricahua chapter, and on the first page there was a duplicate of the illustration shown on the back cover, but this was a picture of the Native's entire body. The upper torso was painted black, and he wore a long woven skirt of Yucca, the caption said. Around his arms were tied sprigs of spruce, and he carried a bough of spruce in one hand. In the other hand was a wand held menacingly, and it was pointed at the reader. The caption explained his dress and that the dance was one to ward off sickness, or heal those during an epidemic.

According to the author, Jerod's dancer was called the "Black One", and was considered very dangerous. The Black One belonged to a larger category of dancers called the Gan impersonators. But the irony was that this dancer did not dance. His purpose was to keep away everything bad. Jerod's hamburger grew cold and forgotten on the coffee table, as he continued to read.

At one point he got up to use the bathroom and on the way back down the hallway he looked through the open door to his bedroom. He saw the "bundle" lying where he had left it, next to his bed. Jerod picked up the bundle and gingerly carried it back to the sofa.

Jerod reached for his malt on the coffee table and found it had turned watery, separated and barely cool. He decided to get a cold soda from the refrigerator when he remembered he had planned to call Linda. He dialed her number from the phone in the living room, and on the eighth ring Linda answered. She had just caught the phone on her way in the door from work.

They only talked for a few minutes. Jerod had told her that he was reading an interesting book, and Linda had encouraged him to get back to it. He hadn't argued, because he suddenly found himself growing very sleepy. He popped the ring on the can of soda, set it down on the coffee table, and untied the shirtsleeves of his bundle. It was the last thing he remembered until much later.

***

Chapter 9

GOLTHLAY

GOLTHLAY

The People reacted to the words of Yellow Bird with shock and dismay. They waited for an immediate reprisal with the certainty their legends had taught them would surely come. The Cha-ja-la, the dance that called on the power of the Mountain People to extricate the sickness, had failed. An outsider had foiled their medicine, and the child who Golthlay had dropped so casually into their midst would bring more of the White Man's evil and pain.

As days passed, and then weeks, more of the clan's people fell ill. Those who suffered the loss of a child or elderly member of their family looked suspiciously at the events that took place on the eve of the Medicine Spirit Dance.

The initial quiet and shock gave way to angry words. At first The People spoke in hushed tones behind Golthlay's back. After all, this was a man of no tolerance, who had already displayed his temper and fierce determination in personal disputes, as well as battles. Others had long spoken of the irony in his name, "The yawning one".

The Elders of the tribe, who were the carriers of wisdom, could never be stilled long. It was their responsibility to speak out and guide their chief. The shaman, too, was one of those who joined the council to discuss these and other more disturbing events. They gathered this morning at the central fire, where wisps of blue smoke and the smell of breakfast cakes still filled the air.

The Chiricahua, now a people displaced and constantly moving, had found some stability on this mountain plateau. They were aware that a permanent home was not possible as long as the White Man and Mexican hunted them, but this secret ledge, so high on the mountain, offered a needed degree of security. It was especially important now that many of their people were weakened from the sickness. Still, it would only be a home until the time their chief ordered them to break camp.

Many joined the council with trepidation. Those who would speak must proceed cautiously, so as not to inflame the temper of their leader. Golthlay was a man who knew his own power; with confidence he presented his arguments first.

"I would remind our people that the supplies we have brought back have put food in the bellies of our braves. It was a successful raid, one that acquires the needed time for our people to recover from the sickness."

"We would not argue with our chief on that account. The People give thanks to Usen for all that the warriors have brought back." Naiche was careful to give a two-edged compliment. Noticeably missing was the direct appreciation of Golthlay's leadership.

Naiche continued, "This White Man's child will bring trouble, and may already have brought much sickness. According to your wife, this very morning Yellow Bird, herself, has taken ill. I say it would be best to be rid of her!"

"No. She is valuable to our people. At the very least we could trade more horses with the White-Eyes for her return," Golthlay pointed out.

Kay-I-Tah contradicted him. "Her yellow hair would be worth more to some men!"

The holy man, Dee-O-Det, who had remained silent, raised his hand to his heart. He looked carefully at Golthlay, and then addressed his chief.

"You have given reasons why the child was brought here, and have stated her usefulness for barter. What are your reasons for her to stay, Golthlay?"

All of those in the council turned their heads to Golthlay. The holy man was asking the question that they had on their minds, for they had noticed their chief's concern for Yellow Bird's welfare, a personal concern usually reserved for family members.

Hadn't they watched as Golthlay chastised his woman, when her treatment of Yellow Bird had been inferior to that of their daughter? Golthlay was aware of the clan's eyes on him. He was equally confused, and yet his pride would not allow for that confession. Until these more recent events, Golthlay had been certain where he stood. He had taken the oath of Netdahe, "death to all intruders". It had always been simple; the intruders were all of those who were not Apache. He saw his interests in terms of race and culture, not as individuals. Survival was dependent on this hard thinking.

It was time for Golthlay to tell of the dream, the dream that had troubled him so. He would have preferred to discuss this alone with Dee-O-Det, but his own fears and disdain for self-contemplation had silenced his tongue. The great warrior, who had never hesitated to rise in fierce defense of his people, now rose hesitantly to speak to them.

"I have something to tell my people that I do not fully understand. I will look to our holy man to interpret my dream, though I can say it spoke to me with the clearness of a stream." Golthlay shifted his weight uneasily, looking first at his feet and then into the eyes of those around him.

"On the night of the Medicine Spirit Dance, I did not close my eyes until the first morning birds had made their call. When I did sleep a dream came to me.

"Yellow Bird came to me in the dream and led me to another place. She was no longer a child, but a grown woman dressed as white women dress. She silently beckoned me to come with her. We flew over the earth, traveling much distance. In one hand she carried the Gan wand, and she pointed to those things she wished me to see. The other hand she kept tightly pressed to her breast, holding something that I could not see.

"This place we flew over, I had never been to. This world was not as we know it. Many people covered the earth. Apaches were only few among the many. These people moved around quickly, like the ants before a rainstorm.

"We traveled far, and I felt the wind rush against me. Great waters and mountains passed beneath us, and we continued through clouds and rain and sunshine. Finally, we came to a range of mountains, and began a fast descent. We landed on a high plateau that towered above the pines, and she led me to a cave. The sun was low in the sky and its light slanted deep into the cave and shone on the inside wall.

"There, with great reverence, Yellow Bird pointed the wand to the talking pictures painted across the wall. The first picture was of our Chiricahua clan and our wikiups. Our people were fat and happy and secure. I knew that this was the way things had been before we ran from the White Man and the Mexican.

"The second picture was about our life now. I knew this because there were fewer of our people, and some lay sick and dying. A great loneliness came over me as I saw the few survivors of our people.

"I felt our impending loss and saw in my heart the annihilation of the Apache. Yellow Bird had no patience with my tears and pointed eagerly to the third picture.

"Here was a great wikiup of the White Man. Children, both White and Apache, were playing in front. They seemed happy enough and well fed. As I drew closer to the painting, I saw that Yellow Bird stood in the doorway of the wikiup, and in her hand was a book of talking pictures.

"When I turned to ask Yellow Bird what was the meaning of this picture, she extended the hand that she had held clutched to her breast. In this hand was a book, the same one in the picture. She looked into my eyes, and I knew that she wanted me to take the book. The next thing I knew I heard the Mourning Dove, and my dream was gone. I felt the early chill and smelled ash cakes cooking on the fire, but still I could not forget what I had seen. Today, two moons since, I still remember."

The People had listened intently, and even now that Golthlay had finished talking they were quiet for some time.

"You should have told us this before," said the holy man. "I will have to think on this and what this vision means to our people."

When even the chief looked chastised, Dee-O-Det added, "You were right not to decide the child's future until now."

The crowd broke up and solemnly went about their day's business. This was not as simple as it had first appeared, and though there were those tribal members who thought the child to be a bad omen, this was a matter for the Elders.

Golthlay walked back to his blanket, where his wife and daughter tended the child with yellow hair. He was uncomfortable in the knowledge that everyone knew his dream, and at the same time he felt some relief. It was not just his problem now. He searched through their belongings and pulled out one of the jugs brought back from the raid. Taking the jug and his rifle, Golthlay mounted his horse and rode off without a word.

***

In the weeks that had passed since Yellow Bird's arrival at the Apache stronghold, she had learned to adapt amazingly well. Her tender age made her pliable in her caretaker's hands. She had learned that crying, or even protesting, was not rewarded. Only on the eve of the Medicine Spirit Dance was her crying even acknowledged, and then it was quickly suffocated.

The curious Apache children soon overcame their shyness and approached Yellow Bird. The children found their own way to communicate. An offering of a strip of jerky or a bowl of water was often the first gesture of friendship. Still there was no indulgence on the part of the adults in the clan, and for the most part the child's care was left to the older girl children.

Those who were able, from the youngest to the oldest, made themselves useful, and though the clan had long been on the run, the only chore not currently part of their lives was farming. They depended now on gathering the foods that grew wild.

Golthlay's daughter was eight years old when Yellow Bird came. She and the other girls of similar age were assigned the duty of gathering pine nuts and supervising Yellow Bird as she learned to help them.

And so the child began to fit in to the clan, eating the foods the Apache ate, playing the games of their children, learning the restraint necessary to find her place in that society. Yellow Bird had sufficiently blocked the memories of cabin life with her first family. There were few memories to haunt her or to cause nightmares.

Only one memory remained bright. As an infant in frontier life, shoes were not a part of dress. Shoes were a necessity for those who needed protection for their feet. Older children wore them to do chores during the winter and, if they were lucky, to go to school. They were not a necessity for the toddler who remained at her mother's side at the kitchen hearth. The purchase of the high-top shoes by Virginia's parents had made a deep impression on Virginia. In her mind's eye she could no longer see her father, weary from work, or her older brother, as he eagerly attempted to keep up with him. She could no longer feel her mother's arms around her as she read to her, but she did have a vague memory of the lilting melodies that her mother had sung on those quiet days so long ago. More clearly, still, she saw the little brown leather shoes sitting in the corner of the room.

Virginia's family of another time and place had purchased them on a rare trip to town. The high-top button shoes were a luxury bought, along with few others, from the profit the ranch had managed this year. Her mother had hesitated, but Virginia's father had said, "No, she'll be helpin' you this winter with chores. I won't have her pampered and spoiled!" That had been the end of her mother's meek protest. Of course, they were purchased a couple of sizes too large. It was a while till winter, and Virginia would grow before they would be needed.

They had been Virginia's treasured possession, sitting new and proper on the wood floor at the foot of her bed, while she spent a summer scampering barefoot about the ranch. On days when there was little to amuse the only small child in an adult family, Virginia would sit on the floor and tug on her oversized shoes. And then her mother would scold and caution her not to wear them, as she would need them soon enough.

This warning had been enough, until the night of the late summer storm. The few drops falling on the dusty porch had quickly become a downpour, and the Arizona sky opened up with blinding light and cracking thunder. Virginia's parents and brother were running from barn to corrals, securing gates and livestock for fear the animals would spook and run.

The three-year-old stood alone on the porch, as long as she could manage, but when the thunder became increasingly loud and she felt her body tremble with the earth beneath her, she put on her new shoes and bolted off the porch to find her mother. The dry desert floor could not absorb the drenching rain and soon large puddles began to pool.

Virginia clumped down the stairs with shoes waggling on the soles of her small feet. In her panic she almost fell headlong into the first puddle. The rain was coming in torrents and a silver sheet fell between Virginia and her family. Alone and frightened, she tried to run, calling to her mother. The hard earth had now turned to a sucking clay, lying deceptively beneath the puddles.

Virginia's first step was swallowed in the mire, as was the next. Frozen in place by fear and mud, the child stood crying until her mother came running to sweep her up into safe arms. Soaking wet, they returned to the safety of the house and left outside the pathetically ruined shoes to scrape clean on a drier day.

Yellow Bird turned restlessly in her sleep and called out "shoes!" She babbled other protests, but this was the only word unrecognizable to Golthlay's wife. There was little doubt that the child had the sickness. She had become progressively worse since the morning. Strangely, she had a red blotchy rash, unlike the others who had fallen sick. Golthlay's wife hoped the elders would soon make a decision about the child. All of their lives were in danger.

***

Golthlay drew on the jug, allowing the liquor to burn out its own fire. He was painfully aware that he had spoken more words before the council than he had ever strung together at one time. For several weeks the dream had weighed heavily on his mind and he had wrestled with the thought of telling his people. It was not the Native way to explain feelings and how could he explain what he did not fully understand? In some ways the child was the White Man's counterpoint to his own character. Where Golthlay was forthright and even brutal in his assessment of the clan's future, he saw this helpless child as a curious symbol of innocent courage.

That Yellow Bird saw Golthlay as her only friend, and had placed her trust in the murderer of her family, was not a fact overlooked by the warrior. She had disarmed him as no enemy had ever done. Golthlay sat on the rock overlooking the valley, and drank until his thoughts became numb.

At some point Dee-O-Det rode up and dismounted quietly. Golthlay offered the holy man the bottle and in silence they proceeded to finish it. The sun crossed the sky, and a mist rose from the earth below before the holy man spoke.

"I, too, have watched this child and wondered if there was a plan. This dream that has visited you was the will of Usen, and Yellow Bird must be a part of Usen's will. You know, as well as I, that the books of talking pictures have meant much to the White Man. Their children go to schools, which prepare them for a different world. Would not our children benefit?

"The ways of this world are changing no matter what we do, Golthlay. We have been pushed from here and from there, but there will be a time when there is no place for our people to run.

"I think that Yellow Bird has a part in teaching our people, in preparing them. She came to you in the dream to show you, our leader, the way, but she cannot fulfill Usen's will if she dies."

Golthlay did not hesitate, "Then you must not let her!"

They did not stay longer, as both the chief and the holy man saw their course of action. When they rode back to camp there was an argument going on among the Elders of the tribe. Three men approached Dee-O-Det, obvious in their attempt to sidestep a confrontation with Golthlay. Golthlay did not seem to notice, as he returned quickly to his own fire.

The holy man was under no illusion. In the democratic manner of reaching tribal decisions the Elders had great influence. They were more than old men bringing their wisdom to counsel the leader of the clan. The Elders were living history. Their stories, told over and over, included their own memories and those of their ancestors. Those who listened were not only entertained by tales of fierce battles and heroic deeds, they learned of the connections of generations past and explanations for their very existence. The world all around them, animal, plant, and mineral, was understood in the context of the life force that remained unseen. Daily life reflected this marriage of trust between humans and earth. The verbal history was an unbroken line of truth.

The Elders did not rewrite history; they were only its witnesses. They saw the holy man's Mountain Spirit Dance as a failure. Was it not true that death was still present? Maybe their holy man was losing his power. The Elders, of whom Dee-O-Det was one, knew that there was no shame in this fact, only shame for one who would deny it. Honesty was still the holy man's most important virtue, for beyond dealings with his own people it was his relationship with the Spirit World that would tolerate no self-deception.

Dee-O-Det sat on the mountain ledge, joined by a circle of his peers, and listened to their words. The holy man lit his pipe and handed it to Naiche, who drew short puffs and then passed it on to the others. Finally, there was silence, for the old men had each said their piece and respectfully awaited the holy man's reply.

"You have told me what you see, and I have listened carefully. However, there is much work for me to do and so you must take leave."

The men were surprised and alarmed. They had expected more discussion and instead they were being dismissed.

***

The holy man watched as the men got up to leave. He felt relief and renewed energy of purpose now that he had made his decision. He knew that he would need this energy, as he had a physical mission before him. The sun was leaving this side of the mountain. It would be too late to start out now, but an early morning departure would have him return that much sooner.

The years had taught him something, he thought. The first, being his own weakness. It would be a strenuous climb, but he would seek out the home of the Mountain People. He would make his appeal in person.

Before he went to sleep he had one errand to make, and so Dee-O-Det made a visit to Golthlay.

The chief was sitting close to the fire, his thoughts somewhere beyond the flames. He turned when he saw his old friend approach and bade him to join him.

"There is something I must do before I can help the girl. I will go up the mountain as Life Giver has instructed me, and when I return I will see the child."

"I am not certain how much time we have," Golthlay informed him. "She has been with fever most of the day and is growing weaker."

Dee-O-Det un-wrapped the crushed herbs and roots taken from the leather pouch that hung at his side. Giving them to Golthlay, he described how they were to be administered.

"Have your woman make a tea, and offer Yellow Bird small amounts of it frequently. It is important that her body is cooled."

Reaching back into the pouch, he unfolded a piece of rawhide that contained another herb. He explained how this was to be made into a poultice and applied to the areas of the child's body where her pulse beat strongest.

Golthlay took the holy man's forearm in his own two hands. Grasping firmly, he said, "I know your power is strong and I will pray for you."

"It is Usen's power that is strong, Golthlay. Pray, instead, that it be given to Yellow Bird."

***

The temporary stronghold did not occupy much land. The conformation of the usable land on the mountain restricted the number and type of dwellings. A wikiup made of poles and grass was an extravagance, and most members of the tribe were living in the cave itself. Their privacy was garnered by constructing simple lean-tos, and a reminder that The People were being hunted and dare not become too comfortable.

An exception was Dee-O-Det's wikiup, as it had other purpose than lodging. There, were the belongings of a holy man, not to be seen by other eyes.

The holy man rose stiffly from his blanket before the first light. He was an old man now, though the Elders' activity was not decided by years but by ability. He still rode with raiding parties, and hunted his own buck each year to renew his medicine power. Before him now was his hardest task, to climb the mountain, to beseech the Mountain People. A holy man with Mountain Spirit power can perform his rite without the need of Gan dancers.

He prepared now to make his pilgrimage. Dee-O-Det pulled back the leather hanging that was the wikiup's door. Tied to a stake, just outside the entrance, was a mule fully packed and saddled, waiting for his journey. Golthlay must have instructed one of the younger braves to prepare the mule sometime during the night. The old man smiled in appreciation of his good friend and swung an arthritic leg across the mule's back.

Once mounted, the old man and the mule broke from camp before there was any sign of tribal stirring. Stars still filled the sky, but there was no moon at this early morning hour. The mule picked his way in the dark, carefully finding the trail that led up the side of the mountain.

Pines hung wickedly from the steep side of the bank on the mule's right. Dee-O-Det held his bow erect to probe the blackness in front of his face. He heard a night hawk screech off in the distance and then from some point even further, he heard its mate answer the call.

***

Chapter 10

JACK OWENS

JACK OWENS

Jack Owens stifled a surge of panic. He hadn't realized their finances had become so out of control. The pile of bills lying in front of him was indisputable proof; that, and the call from the bitch at the credit-card center. Jack stared across the new mahogany dining room table, the one that was three payments in arrears, and focused mindlessly on the doll collection behind the glass of the "in hock" china cabinet. There were beads of perspiration lining his brow, and even the obscure reflection in the glass revealed the pallor of his skin. He looked half dead and felt worse.

He had yelled a string of obscenities when Lisa had brought in the newest stack of credit card receipts. What in the hell had she been thinking? She had maxed out each piece of plastic! Jack could imagine her at the counter of her favorite boutique, when the cashier quietly took her aside to tell her that her credit card was at its limit, and would she like her to put back the white brocade suit? He was certain that Lisa had found her way around that one with some inane comment about the bank's inefficiency. She had obviously solved the nuisance problem, because the suit now hung in the closet with all the other expensive clothes. This particular credit card had a new balance of $4,864.39; so had the woman in charge of his account said, on the phone, several minutes earlier.

If he could have been fair, Jack would have admitted that his spending habits were no less frugal than Lisa's. From the BMW in the garage, private schools for the kids, to evenings out at the best restaurants, he had contributed his part to living beyond their apparent means. But it hadn't been apparent. He had worn blinders.

His job had paid well, and when it wasn't enough, Lisa borrowed from her father. There was no way this could be happening to them. He worked hard and they earned good money. They deserved a good life, for crying out loud!

So, they were a little overextended. A home-equity loan would have caught them up, and satisfied all the small chumps whining for their money. Jack had been so certain of the loan when he entered the bank to meet with Ms. Caulfield.

***

The prim little plaque on her desk had read Linda Caulfield, Loan Officer. She was actually a sexy looking blonde, which was sure to make this nasty bit of paper work almost worth his one-hundred-twenty-mile drive from Tucson. Jack introduced himself with an instant smile, and Ms. Caulfield returned an all-business handshake.

Linda Caulfield asked him a few polite questions. Mostly to put the sucker at ease, Jack thought. He knew the score. He understood verbal manipulation, or diplomacy as it was probably called, during the behind-the-scenes sales meetings of the bank's loan officers.

Yeah, well, he could hustle, too. Jack did his best to remain calm and cool as he carefully picked his way around the broad's subtle questions.

"Oh, you live and work in Tucson, I see. So does my brother. My fiancé is working there, too. The economy is rather depressed right now, isn't it?" Ms. Caulfield looked at him quizzically, waiting for his reply.

Jack reminded himself that there was no way she could know that Sin Par Space Technology was planning layoffs. No one knew this, not even Dan. The misdirected paper work, that had accidentally found its way to his desk, had not left before Jack had scanned it for any pertinent information. It paid to be on your toes. This top-level memo, intended for department heads, instructed a twenty-percent reduction in personnel, across the board. That would translate to one out of five engineers in their department. He did not like the odds.

Looking out for numero uno was second nature to Jack. He maneuvered through the chitchat as if it were a minefield, and found the only surprise was that Ms. Caulfield had suddenly lost her sex appeal. She finally brought out the paper work, and Jack was left alone with a cup of coffee to fill out the financial application.

Jack looked over the questions suspiciously. This had to be done carefully. He did his best to imply hidden income, with reference to accounts on which he was only a signer. When it came to credit references, Jack kept them minimal, betting they wouldn't all report balances to a credit-reporting agency. Personal references were kept short, too: his mother, Lisa's father, and in the place of friends, just Dan and Ryann Thearle. The less information, the better, he thought.

When he finished the forms, Linda Caulfield all but dismissed him with the empty promise that he would be hearing from her on the loan's outcome within forty-eight hours. Jack found his inner fear replaced with a smoldering hate. How dare this broad think she was better than he? What could her salary be, anyway? She was going to string him along, sure as shit. Didn't she know who she was dealing with here?

Jack felt his shirt collar rub irritatingly against his flushed neck. As soon as he was out the bank door, he yanked at his tie and loosened what felt like a noose around his neck.

***

No, this was not the cinch he thought it would be. His appointment had been Tuesday and this was Thursday afternoon, and he still hadn't heard. What the hell? Well, he thought, if Muhammad won't come to the mountain ... Maybe, he had to let this broad know who was boss, put a few screws to her job.

"Are you all right?" Lisa's voice startled him so that Jack's hand knocked over his full cup of cold coffee.

"Crap! Look what you made me do!" The coffee had spilled over the paper work and was soon dripping down the side of the tablecloth, on to the rug.

Hurriedly, Lisa went to the kitchen to get a towel, calling back to Jack, "Lift up the table cloth, so that the coffee won't stain the rug!"

"Oh sure, protect the God damn rug! Don't you see what's going on here, Lisa? I'm trying to figure out how to pay your God damn bills!"

Jack looked down at the soggy pile of receipts and watched as the ink ran and numbers blurred. Lisa came back in the room and began dabbing at the pooled coffee, oblivious to his words. Jack grabbed her arm and spun her around.

Screaming now, he spat his words into her face. "Don't you understand anything, bitch? We're bankrupt if I don't get this loan!"

Jack was hurting her. She could feel his fingers dig deep into her arms. But more frightening than this pain were Jack's eyes. They darted wildly around the room, as if looking for something to pin down and -- torture? The tic that Lisa had noticed developing on the left side of Jack's face during the last few weeks was now an uncontrolled twitch.

"Stop it, the kids will hear you!"

Lisa was still more concerned with the kids walking in on this scene than her own danger. Her voice mustered enough authority to break up Jack's rage, at least momentarily. Lisa felt Jack expel his breath and relax his grip. Nervously, she backed up several steps out of his reach. She knew that when he was like this, there was no way that she could reason with him. Even now, she wondered if he had ever been like *this*.

Though Jack had released her, he was still possessed. His face, his whole body, was wired in tension. He didn't seem to know she was there. Lisa confronted the fact that, indeed, he might have lost his mind. There was no point in staying here in the room with him and risk finding out. She would quietly get the children and leave.

She admitted to herself that she was frightened, but this was not the time to show fear. Where would she go today? With enough time to think Lisa knew that she would probably make the decision that would change their lives forever. In the meantime, until she could talk to her father in Colorado, she had to get the kids and get out of here.

Jack was rummaging through the damp papers, mumbling to himself, and no longer seemed aware of Lisa's presence. Lisa quietly slipped out the sliding glass door to the patio and began looking for the kids.

***

Dan made up his mind to return to work on Wednesday. He couldn't help but feel some guilt because he was genuinely worried. Mandy's actions had been very strange. It wasn't just that she was sick. In fact the rash seemed much better, now that they had addressed the itch with calamine lotion. She hadn't vomited anymore either, but the fever would recur unpredictably and, when it did, Mandy would begin to babble incoherently.

They had spent a restless night, frequently waking to sounds from Mandy's bedroom. One such time he knew Ryann was still asleep, as her rhythmic breathing continued uninterrupted, and so he got up to check on Mandy. When he reached the door to Mandy's bedroom he heard Slouch growl a low warning. He opened the door and announced his presence by softly calling to Slouch. Maybe the dog was dreaming or just overprotective. In either case, Slouch didn't stop growling when Dan entered. Dan thought, whatever the dog's beef was, it wasn't with him.

As he drew closer to the bed he heard Mandy talking in her sleep. Actually, it was more like mumbling. Dan couldn't make out a single word. When he bent over to feel her forehead, she felt feverish. He and Ryann had agreed to record Mandy's intake of medicine on a little note pad on the table by her bed. Because both parents were sharing in the nursing, there wouldn't be any danger of overdosing if they recorded what they gave her and when. Dan checked the last time she had Tylenol and noted it had been more than five hours ago. He tried to wake her gently.

The soft light from the lamp by her bed only enhanced her vulnerability. Mandy looked so frail. Dan helped her to sit up so that she could drink from the glass. She swallowed the pills he held to her mouth, and Dan saw that she was completely disoriented. She obeyed like a zombie, with no recognition. Dan did not like the feeling this gave him. Somehow it was not the same as the times he had to carry her from the car when they came home late from a movie. That kind of drowsy, warm slumber was part of Mandy's implicit trust in her father's safe arms. This little girl was a blind prisoner in a foreign body. She did not know that it was her dad in the room, Dan was sure of that. Even more disturbing was the fact that she didn't seem to care.

He lowered her head to the pillow and tucked in the blanket around her. There was a cool breeze flowing across Mandy's bed, and Dan got up to see if the only window in the bedroom was open. He was surprised to find it closed. When he turned to cross the room, he tripped clumsily over the dog. Slouch's low rumblings turned to open hostility. The dog's lips curled back from his teeth and he growled a challenge.

Dan thought Slouch was looking straight at him. He felt a moment of fear and yet almost instantaneous comprehension. It was a knee-jerk reaction and certainly understandable. This was instinctive behavior, and Dan obligingly backed out of the way. Slouch's eyes did not follow him, however, but were fixed on some point of the bear's tea party in the corner of the room. Dan, too, looked at the miniature red table and chairs, but saw nothing out of the ordinary. He felt the hair on his forearms stand at attention and had a sudden desire to flee the room. Dan fought his own instincts and determined to put the dog out instead.

Dan went to the door and ordered Slouch to follow him. Twice he called his name sharply, and twice the dog apparently heard nothing. Finally Dan yelled, "Slouch!" and the dog blinked, turning to see what caused the ruckus. It was as if he had just come out of a trance, Dan thought.

Once out of the room, Slouch meekly followed Dan to the kitchen's backdoor and outside, into the dark.

***

The night became a blur of other sounds. Dan remembered hearing Ryann get up once. He went into Mandy's room one more time, but her fever was down and he thought it was a good sign. When he checked the clock this last trip, he saw there was no sense in going back to bed, and decided to put on the coffeepot instead.

Ryann grinned sleepily at him.

"Did you smell the coffee?" Dan asked.

"Yeah, I didn't realize it was this late. You should have waked me."

"Well, it's back to work, you know. I'm the lucky one, I guess. You think you can handle it?"

Dan was sitting at the kitchen table nursing his second cup of coffee. Ryann came over and found a seat on his lap. She lazily draped her arm around Dan's neck and hugged him.

"It's all downhill now, don't you think?" Ryann searched his face. "Mandy felt cool when I checked on her last. I think she is going to be just fine." Ryann seemed convinced.

"I'm leaving the car for you, anyway, just in case. That was Jack on the phone, and he agreed to drive today, though it would probably be best if he would let me drive. The guy is a nervous wreck lately!" Dan felt his leg begin to fall asleep and reluctantly squirmed.

"Some romantic you are." Ryann teased, but bounced up, nevertheless.

***

Between a sleepless night, too much coffee, and Jack's driving, Dan wished he had some antacids on him. He searched his pockets in vain and only found a dime, two nickels, and a folded piece of notepaper. Instead of staring at the road in preparation for what he imagined would be their certain deaths, he concentrated on relaxing his brake foot, and studied the sketch for Mandy's palm house.

Actually, it was going to look more like a Native dwelling. A wikiup was what he had read they were called. Very southwestern and very practical, he thought.

This wild, wild west was really doing a trip on him lately. Dan had enough of western hazards, like Valley Fever! It was hard to find anything romantic about an "Old West" that deposited diseases in the soil for future generations of innocent children. But he knew he would salvage his outlook once Mandy felt better.

During this morning's commute Jack had been rattling on about interest rates and other financial matters. Dan thought there wasn't much point in following this conversation too closely. As usual, it seemed Jack was talking to himself. Dan took a pencil from his shirt pocket and made several corrections to his drawing of the wikiup.

The car radio was tuned to an energetic pair of disc jockeys, and with the windows rolled shut Dan didn't hear the train whistle for many crucial moments. When Dan looked up, he saw that Jack still hadn't heard and was completely oblivious to the blinding red light ahead. They were heading for the railroad crossing and Jack had no intention of stopping.

There was an instant when Jack turned to him, his eyes completely off the road, and Dan sensed that he had just asked him a question. Then all time and all sound stopped as Dan reached over, fumbling his leg around the occupied accelerator, and slammed his own foot on the brake. With both hands he yanked the steering wheel a full half-turn in his own direction.

The BMW responded instantly. The car went into a slide, never quite losing complete traction. More like a controlled drift, Dan thought. At the end of what seemed like forever, they came to a complete stop parallel to the tracks, maybe even on the tracks. And then before that thought fully registered its fear, the train was roaring by, just inches away from Jack's window.

Hideously, train wheels clacked noisily on and on against the metal sections of rail, while Jack and Dan sat frozen in their seats considering their close call. It was a long train, and Dan was amazed to find he was thinking about its cargo, as the smell of sun-ripened cantaloupes filled the car.

The rest of the trip was uneventful ... the way silence most likely follows a near-disaster, Dan thought. After his heart had quit pounding, anger began to fill the void left by fear.

Jack was crazy! What else could explain this last bit of insanity? Dan realized how close he had come to losing his own life at the hands of an idiot. Whatever problems Jack had, whatever blinders he was wearing in regard to life, by default they had almost become Dan's death sentence. Wasn't it rather like the frying pan calling the kettle black? He couldn't get around the fact that he was ultimately responsible for knowing that Jack was irresponsible.

Dan felt a good deal older. He had a strange feeling that Jack's actions on the job were just as careless. He certainly knew they were self-serving. Jack was functioning like a plane without a pilot, and Dan made a decided point to keep his eyes and ears open. It was time he took a more active role in his own survival.

***

Though he felt haggard, when Dan sat down at the mainframe computer terminal, he began to feel like his old self. The morning was soon behind him and his work absorbed him.

There were five engineers, whose names were listed on the door of the Engineering Department. The room itself was a cool, over-sized, dimly lit area that accommodated separate cubicles for Dan, Jack, and the other three engineers. There, during an average day they would create designs using the "tools" selected from a palette. Large, brightly lit screens became the drawing boards, and the "mouse" the pen, the instrument which created the first drawings. NASTRAN, or the linear statistical analysis code, was the software program that calculated the stress capabilities, which would determine whether the design could go on to production.

It was a comfortable, informal atmosphere that encouraged brainstorming and cooperative projects and still provided the space necessary for individuals to create independently.

On one side of Engineering was an equally large room that housed the CAD, computer-aided-design, operators. These operators converted the engineers' drawings to manufacturing designs for production. The final product in this department was the working vellums runoff on the central plotter.

Management offices were adjacent to the other side of the Engineering Department, with a main entrance off the corridor, but there was also a single door that led directly to Operations, located behind Dan's work area. At 9:45 that door opened and Mrs. Palmer, the secretary to the Operations manager, discreetly motioned to Dan Thearle that the boss would like a word with him.

Lester Gains had been with Sin Par Space Technology for eighteen years, and was an example of the kind of company loyalty fostered by the plant. Generally, there was little turnover. Contracts came and went, but for the most part work had been constant, keeping Sin Par's employees sure of a paycheck. In busier times there was considerable overtime, and it was expected that employees would accept the longer hours and adapt it to their family life. The pay-off was that during lean times there were few layoffs.

Dan was ushered into Lester Gain's office and offered a chair facing the Operations Manager's desk.

"Dan, I apologize for sneaking you out in this manner. I wanted to speak to you in confidence and thought it best we didn't draw too much attention out front." Lester gestured to the door and the Engineering room on the other side.

"There are going to be some cuts made, inevitable, with the budget and all. I just want you to know that your job at Sin Par is secure. I know that you have the least seniority in your department, but we like your work. We like you!" Lester Gains smiled openly and leaned back in his chair.

There had been little time for Dan to become apprehensive and it dawned on him that this had been part of the plan.

"I appreciate that, sir."

Gains was visibly relieved, which Dan found curious. The two men studied each other's faces a moment, and then Gains leaned across the desk to admit his real concern.

"Actually, there are rumors going around, and that's because certain information is reaching the wrong hands. I don't know whether you've heard any, but I thought this little visit might prevent some needless worry. What really concerns me is this matter of misplaced information. It could be the tip of the iceberg, you understand?"

Dan's expression said he didn't and Gains was blunt. "This is not the first memo to fall in the wrong hands. The problem is we don't know whose hands. All I'm saying is keep your eyes and ears open."

When Dan was seated in front of his terminal again, he couldn't help but think, those had been his own exact words of warning, to his self.

***

Chapter 11

A POINT IN TIME

A POINT IN TIME

He told himself he was dreaming, but there wasn't any more time to wonder. Jerod was yanked from the sofa into a black hole. He was moving very fast, or everything was moving by him very fast. It was hard to tell. It was impossible to tell, because he was falling and his instinct had kicked in to survive. His arms and legs flung out from his body in a frantic attempt to right himself, to find something to grab on to, but there was no resistance, nothing there when he reached, just the "rushing" that continued to fly past him.

When he found his flailing body had nothing to grasp, he slowly began to accept his weightless state. He couldn't hear his own scream and so he finally quit screaming. He couldn't feel and after awhile he gave up feeling. Reality wasn't altered, it was missing. There was no way to tell how much time had passed. There was nothing with which to measure it.

He fought uselessly for some time. Fear did that. But Jerod grew tired, even weary of the fear. It was then, when his heart quit jumping wildly in his chest and began to settle down to a noisy *thump*-thump, that he began to remember Vietnam.

It had been the same way in Nam; the immobilizing fear had glued his splayed limbs fast to the jungle floor beneath him. There, too, he had only found release from this paralysis when he allowed his mind to leave his body. Lying there, under fire, for what seemed like an eternity, his mind did what any good soldier would do under similar odds, it retreated.

With his inner self safe and removed, he began to look at the predicament. He remembered using that very word -- predicament. It somehow blunted the urgency.

Jerod tried it now. He allowed himself to think of the science projects, where a volunteer would enter an artificial environment with no sensual stimuli. Wasn't the purpose to determine the effects on the mind? This thought became an avenue to complete his own detachment, and Jerod found he was focusing on the only sensation, the "rushing". It was like flying, but there was no wind. There was a sense of speed and yet no physical traveling. Was it time? Was the "rushing" a kind of time machine?

And then, as if making reentry, the blackness became the blue sky and rugged mountains, and the rushing became a beautifully quiet day. Jerod's sudden awareness of all five senses was overpowering: the sharp contrasts of color and textures, green pines on a rocky hillside, the wonderful smells of evergreen, and just a hint of smoke. He was back. This was the real world, but the only thing familiar was that it was real.

Not thirty feet in front of him, a Native crouched in front of a fire, poking at embers with a stick. Jerod heard voices and looked further up the hillside. There were other Natives, women, children, and men ... some moving about, others quietly at work ... all oblivious to him. He felt aware and yet not exposed. It was a strange paradox. Jerod found he could see, smell, and hear ... and he was sure he could feel and taste ... but, there was no sense of self. He wondered if he was invisible.

The Native turned around slowly and faced him. And then Jerod knew he was visible, at least to the man who stood before him now. The Native seemed equally surprised, but addressed him nevertheless.

"Oh, Great Spirit, this is what you have sent me?" Golthlay was shaken. He had asked Usen to intervene, and was humbled with His answer.

Jerod heard the Native speak, but his lips weren't moving. His words were in English, clear and distinct. Jerod looked around. There was no one else in this clearing. The words had to be meant for him, and though the Native spoke loud enough to be overheard by the others on the hill, they didn't seem to notice.

The two men stared at each other, Golthlay standing beside the fire and Jerod at a distance. Jerod was wearing blue jeans and a faded red t-shirt with a picture of an eagle in full flight on the front. Golthlay's eyes took in all of this, as well as Jerod's Nike tennis shoes and socks.

Jerod was familiar with the Native's dress, but was more shocked at being here in this setting. He studied the man's face. It was harsh. He would have described it as cruel, with its brow furrowed deeply over intense dark eyes.

"Who are you?" he asked. Jerod realized that his voice, too, was coming from his mind and not his vocal chords.

"They call me Golthlay," he answered obediently. "You have answered my prayer!" At the corners of the Native's eyes and mouth there appeared the first hint of vanquished pain.

Jerod was terribly confused. It was as if he had walked into a theater midway through a movie. Still there was something in the man's presence, the clear linear reality of this peaceful scene, which calmed him. There was no doubt in his mind that this was happening, he just needed time to catch up.

"Prayer, what is your prayer?" Jerod asked.

"That you intervene, Great One ... that you help our Holy Man cure the child. I beseech you to help us fulfill the dream ..."

Golthlay's voice trailed off in a litany, and Jerod understood that he was being addressed as some sort of god. Those were almost the same words he had heard before. The big question, "Was this scene real or imagined?" again begged an answer, but Jerod put it out of his mind for now. It would be useless torment, he knew. He was here and he was determined to find out why.

"What do you want of me, Golthlay?" Jerod took several tentative steps forward. When he saw his movements did not cause alarm, he drew in closer to the fire.

"Many of my people are sick with the coughing disease. You have sent a white child to us, and have shown me how she is to help our people. But, she is sick, also, and may die before Dee-O-Det returns from the Mountain People. I do not have the power to help her. The Holy Man may not. Usen sent you!" The Native ended his explanation triumphantly.

Jerod wondered if the man could read his mind as easily as he could hear his unspoken words. If so, he was in big trouble. Golthlay was expecting either a miracle or a doctor, and it looked like this was going to be a house call.

He thought about telling him things were not as they seemed, that he wasn't a god, or even a medicine man, but he knew there was little chance of getting by with it. Jerod would have to explain why he was here, and he didn't have the answer to that one.

Jerod stood there, awkwardly toeing the ground with his tennis shoe. Golthlay didn't seem aware of his inadequacy and beckoned for him to follow, as he walked off in the direction of the others.

Maybe he'd better follow along. Even dreams had solutions, he thought. Jerod walked behind the man, up a well-worn path that crisscrossed the side of the mountain. They passed Natives along the way, but no one paid any attention to Jerod. When they reached the summit, they came on to a huge plateau. Caves lined the backside of the ledge, and in the recesses Jerod could see people working at different tasks.

They continued past a woman weaving a basket and others grinding acorns, to a place where a woman was attending a small child. The woman was applying some sort of poultice to the child's forehead. Even here, no one looked at Jerod, but went about their activities completely unaware.

"White Spirit, see Yellow Bird is failing fast." Golthlay sighed in apparent anguish, and dropped to his knees beside the child.

The woman withdrew to tend the fire several feet away, and Jerod moved in closer to see. The girl couldn't have been more than three or four years old. She appeared very thin, and Jerod thought her age might be deceiving. Blonde wisps of damp hair and some mixture of ground herbs matted the child's brow. Her pale face was spotted with a blotchy rash, and she thrashed about, as if from fever. It looked, to Jerod, like some sort of delirium.

Jerod placed his hand on her brow. She was burning up. Almost immediately her arms stopped flailing, and the child lay quietly beneath his hand. Jerod looked up and his eyes met Golthlay's. This was all too much. He saw this scene as one from an old Tarzan movie where the white doctor cured the dying native and saved the day.

"Wait a minute, here, Golthlay, this is just a coincidence." Jerod was pleading to the man's logic. For just a moment he thought it was possible.

"Oh, Great White Spirit stay with her until the Shaman returns!" cried Golthlay.

"Oh, great!" thought Jerod.

***

Again, there was the "rushing", and though Jerod's other senses had shut down, a terrible feeling of vertigo became his center of focus. He fought waves of nausea, and at the same time found comfort in the fact that he had something to battle. It was endless, endless.

Whump! Jerod felt that. He looked up and saw the coffee table and realized that he must have fallen off the couch. His head was throbbing, unmercifully. Rather than test the damage, Jerod contemplated his position on the floor, wedged between two pieces of furniture. Light was streaming in the living room window, which was beyond understanding.

What time was it, anyway? Jerod struggled to get up and his head screamed in protest. His hand went to his head and he pressed his palm firmly on the swollen area. It relieved the pain. He sat down on the sofa and waited for the dizziness to stop. When things quit swimming, he took his hand away and saw his own blood mixed with pieces of green leaves.

He had brought it with him. Jerod stared at his hand and thought of where it had last rested, on the child's brow.

***

A consistency was revealing itself. Whatever the explanation for Jerod's "time warps", there were similarities. He was visiting a time and place belonging to Native Americans, and according to Pete's library, specifically Chiracahui, the "i" ending was plural, the book had explained. Of course, there was the real possibility that his reading had been suggestive. Jerod had to dismiss the idea, because the conclusion rested on the premise that these were dreams. He supposed they could be hallucinations, however.

There was now an accumulation of information. Jerod couldn't put it out of his mind and he couldn't forget it. But he could make further inquiry. It was late afternoon when he checked the clock the first time. He dug into Pete's books and lost himself for hours more.

When his pounding head wouldn't let him read anymore, he decided to shower and eat something, but not before he made his list. Jerod decided to make notes about the trip, of everything that happened on the other side of "rushing". He might forget something that could be important in learning what was happening. He began writing with no particular order in mind, and was surprised at how quickly his list grew.

1) Golthlay
2) Shaman
3) coughing disease
4) Yellow Bird
5) White Spirit
6) Mountain Spirit
7) Usen
8) the caves
9) the herbs
10) the rash

There was more, Jerod was sure, but he would add to it as he remembered. He felt just a little foolish. This was undeniably an attempt to make order out of chaos, yet somehow making the list had helped. But now he was beat, and it was time he took care of himself.

***

Time was completely at odds with Jerod. He wasn't really sure what day it was, and wouldn't have known the hour without a clock. It could be worse, he thought, such as his trip to another century. Jerod didn't have any interest in marking time with the usual interruptions of life. If he was hungry he ate. Never mind the fact that eggs sounded good at two in the morning. He only answered to himself.

Unfortunately, it wasn't the same way when he was tired. Sleep did not come easy. Over the next couple of days Jerod wrestled with his pillow and frequently gave up trying. Eventually he'd get up, put on his old bathrobe, and make a pot of coffee. He'd sit at the kitchen table, staring blurry-eyed at the book before him, and wait for the day to begin. He was looking for answers and there was this gut feeling that it would be on the next page, or maybe in the next book.

He had forced himself to face up to the dilemma of his business, and called Rick and Bill. It was understood that they were on their own this week, unless there was an emergency. This didn't prevent the phone from ringing, however. More than once Jerod picked up the receiver and forced his self to answer congenially, only to hear a computerized sales pitch as a reply. It finally dawned on him to turn on the phone's message recorder and remove this tie to civilization. Once a day Jerod listened to his messages, and realized how dull his social life had become.

The newspaper thumped against the front door, the only interruption to Jerod's monkish life, and it brought him out of his trance. He stepped out on the porch and felt the promise of rain. Huge thunderheads had moved in over the desert. The mammoth cumuli were massing together quickly.

Jerod stood there exhilarated. Wind was gusting about the yard and it carried the scent of rain. It reminded him of fishing trips and a less complicated life. A painful nostalgia settled about him like a suffocating blanket, as he remembered those good times with Mikey, long before the war.

Oh, God, he missed him. The two had been inseparable. Mikey was two years older and Jerod's best friend. They had never envied the kids that lived in town, because they had each other. The old ranch off the dusty road had provided all the entertainment possible for two brothers with such gargantuan imaginations. Days just like this were the playground.

It was no big deal for Mikey to say "Come on, Jerod! Get your pole and let's go to the creek!" The creek was on their property, after all. There they would spend lazy summer afternoons fooling around on the banks of the creek, catching tadpoles, rock-hopping across the shallow parts, and swimming below the falls.

When they would finally collapse, laughing and wet, on the green grass, the two would look up and watch the rolling thunderheads. Every day was more of the same; they never caught a fish, and in blew the clouds every afternoon, threatening a rain that never came. And it was perfect.

Jerod could close his eyes and almost feel his brother next to him. His sweaty little body that smelled of creek, excitement, and licorice, all wrapped up in one. He felt his eyes burn with tears as he fought the anguish the memories always delivered.

Mikey had been drafted into the Vietnam War. Jerod didn't have that excuse. He willingly followed, and on the day he completed his boot camp training at Fort Ord, his father had called. The telegram had come, his dad had finally said through tears and agonizing pauses that had driven Jerod almost out of his mind. He had wanted to reach through the phone and strangle the words from his father's throat. Mikey was gone. Jerod's hero, his brother, was gone.

And then because it was too late to stop the madness, Jerod began his own two-year tour of duty in Vietnam, and the war finished off what his brother's death had begun.

Jerod had been caught off guard and a shot of anger ran through him. Smells were like that. There was no time to prepare for the memory, which bubbled to the surface. Almost like the "rushing", Jerod thought, or even the "something more". He felt very used.

***

Most of Peter Caulfield's collection of books was strewn about the living room floor. Jerod had gone about the task methodically. When the mask had been the only clue, he had searched and found the answer in the books on Native Americans. He had found the explanation in the chapters on the Chiricahua Apache. Now that he had the name "Golthlay" he thought those same chapters would be the place to begin.

Golthlay was everywhere, many times spelled differently. Several books referred to him as Goyathlay and a few others as Gokhlayeh. Only one translated the meaning as "the yawning one", but all of them referred to his English name, "Geronimo".

When Jerod first realized that this was the man, the Native who had implored him to save a child, he was stunned by the man's humanity. Wasn't this the Apache savage who had a drinking problem and massacred early settlers? It was hard to reconcile what he knew firsthand with the Native's reputation. The image wouldn't die easily. Still, he had now read enough about Native Americans to know that the old westerns he had rented from the video store were not exactly an accurate portrayal of southwestern history.

He pictured Golthlay's eyes from memory. Jerod could still feel their intensity, as though they were burning through him. Several pictures that he saw in books did little to confirm Jerod's version of this supposed wild man, except for those haunting eyes. In one photograph he rode in an open car, a 1906 Pierce

Arrow, and wore a silk top hat. But then he turned the page and recognized another photograph as his Apache warrior.

To be fair, Jerod realized that if the average reader were to see this photograph, he would believe the worst about the man. Golthlay posed defiantly with his rifle and looked completely capable of murder. Both versions were at odds with Jerod's appraisal of the man, and yet there was something there of each.

Jerod became so intrigued with the stories about Golthlay that he finally had to force himself to break away. It was evening and he could hear the low rumbling of thunder off in the distance. He went out on the porch and sat in one of two wicker chairs to watch the light show covering the western sky. Lightning briefly illuminated the far-off mountains, and Jerod thought of the place he had visited, Golthlay's home.

The more he read, the more Jerod felt he was on the right path. The percentage of instinct to fact was weighing heavily in favor of the latter. He could actually feel a shift in balance, like the right brain - left brain theory. Strange, he thought, he had to trust his instincts in order to discover the facts. Though he was no longer fighting it, no longer berating himself as either drunk or insane, he did feel a great urgency to discover ... discover what, he wondered.

The phone rang, and forgetting the recording that would kick in after four rings, Jerod sprinted through the doorway to answer it.

"Hello…"

"Jerod? This is Bill Martinez. How are you doing?"

"Bill! Man, I'm glad you called. So much is happening!"

***

Chapter 12

VALLEY FEVER

VALLEY FEVER

Ryann wasn't certain what was troubling Dan. If it was Mandy, she could understand. She had spent her first day alone with their daughter since her doctor appointment, and it had been a bizarre experience. The fever had spiked oddly at different times during the day and when it did Mandy had been delirious. Dan was concerned about Mandy, but there was something else on his mind. He had come home, but his thoughts were elsewhere.

When all else fails, try the direct approach, Ryann thought.

"What's the matter, guy?" Ryann stopped in the midst of cleaning off the dinner dishes, and folded the dishtowel unnecessarily. "Don't tell me there isn't anything, Dan. I know better."

There were those brown eyes that Dan couldn't lie to, and he knew he didn't have a chance in hell. He hadn't wanted to tell Ryann about his day, she really had enough to handle. Whatever made him think that, however noble the purpose, he could conceal anything from this woman? Dan reached across the table and covered her hand with his.

"Okay, already! Anything you say, officer," Dan chided her, and her expression softened.

"Jack almost killed yours truly, for starters. His mind doesn't seem to be with us anymore. We almost collided with a train this morning."

"Oh, Dan! What happened?"

"He was blabbing away. You know how he talks constantly about getting ahead, and lately about getting a loan. Anyway, he wasn't paying attention to traffic. Didn't see the crossing light, didn't hear the bell or the train. At the last minute I grabbed the steering wheel. It was a close one. Too damn close!

"Sometimes I wonder if we really know Jack. I guess what I'm asking myself is *why* do we know him?"

"A good question," Ryann said. "When he and Lisa come over, it's always uncomfortable. Different strokes for different folks, maybe, but we just don't share the same interests. Or maybe values is a better word," she added. "It certainly can't be for Mandy's sake. Look how differently they play, Dan."

Dan thought about the early materialism fostered on the Owens' kids, how they were constantly comparing clothes and toys. Mandy seemed like the only real child of the three. She enjoyed her world of make believe and her imagination could transform the simplest thing into a favorite toy. Like the box in which the VCR had come.

For at least a week this packing box had been a school bus. The sound of the scooting, thumping box making its way down the hallway had driven Dan nuts, but he never said a word, because the unspoken truth was he respected this creativeness, this ability his daughter had to amuse herself.

Tracy and Thad were of a different breed. The Owens' children had to be entertained. The strange thing was that Mandy didn't mind a bit. Even when they were together, Mandy went on with whatever game she had invented. She'd ask them if they wanted to play, and when they didn't show any interest, she'd happily return to her own fun. She held no hypocrisy regarding her interests and therefore felt no need to sacrifice them to others.

"Maybe Mandy is smarter than we are," Ryann said. "Friendships should be based on more than a matter of convenience. Other than ride sharing, our two families don't have much in common."

Dan could see her thinking was following his.

"There is something else. Lester Gains called me in today. He said there was going to be a layoff, but he assured me it wouldn't affect us. Pretty good news, considering I have the least seniority in Engineering.

"He was also feeling me out. I got the feeling he wants me to watch Jack. Nothing specific, but he just told me to keep my eyes open." Dan was leaning back precariously on two legs of the chair. He leaned forward and the sudden noise startled Ryann.

"Babe, I think it's time we got a second car!"

***

They had agreed there would be no more risks. Dan called Jack that evening and tried to convey diplomatically his reasons for no longer riding to work with him. He put the emphasis on the new car for which he and Ryann were planning to shop this weekend.

"Yeah, Jack, I think it's best that Ryann have a car, especially with Mandy sick and everything. We agreed I'd drive the new one, better gas mileage, you know. You're welcome to ride with me, of course."

Jack wasn't buying any of it. Dan thought his voice had a higher pitch, and an edge of defensiveness he hadn't heard before.

"It's probably best. Dropping you off is really out of my way. Anyway, I'll see you at work, right?"

Right. It was a short conversation and Dan was thankful it was over. Dan had just hung up when he heard Mandy call him. He went to check on her, and was surprised to see his daughter sitting in the middle of the bed, looking every bit the miniature princess in her imaginary realm of billowing blankets and pillows. It was encouraging to see roses in Mandy's cheeks, and Dan was relieved she recognized her old dad.

"How you doing, kid?" he asked.

"Okay. I heard you talking, Daddy, and I knew you were home from work. I hear real good now. My rash is going away. See?" Mandy held out her hands, palms up, inviting an inspection.

"Great, the rash is fading, huh? You don't feel hot, either." This was a relief. Dan hugged her gently and smiled.

"Will you read me a story, Daddy?"

"How about tonight, at bedtime?" Dan asked.

"All right," Mandy answered tolerantly, and then as an afterthought added, "Maybe I'll tell you one."

***

Ryann said she thought it best to bring Mandy's dinner to her for at least another night. She didn't seem as satisfied with her progress as Dan had been. A role reversal from what Dan remembered the first night.

"Sometimes she looks like she is almost well, but then other times she doesn't even recognize me. It's frightening."

"What did the doctor say?"

"Dr. Harrison called back this afternoon. He didn't seem too concerned about the fever. Said it might go on for some time, but it was important for Mandy to have a lot of fluids. He thought the biggest worry was respiratory problems and the possibility of the disease disseminating to other organs. It's not likely, though."

Dan didn't think this was the time to refer to Mandy's strange statements. Ryann had enough on her hands, and besides the fever was probably the explanation.

They cleaned up the kitchen together, and Dan went to keep his promise to Mandy.

"All right, what do you want me to read?"

"Make up one first, Daddy." Mandy patted the bedclothes smooth, making a place for Dan to sit beside her.

"How about our playhouse? Would you like to see what it's going to look like?" Dan took the sketch from his pocket and showed her the drawing. He explained how they would take palm branches from the large tree in the front yard and use them for the roof. They would provide the shade, he said.

Mandy scowled at the drawing a moment and then said, "It's not supposed to look like that! Let me have the pencil, Daddy. I'll show you."

Dan obliged, and watched as his daughter made sweeping corrections on the paper. Her face was fixed in concentration, and a pink tongue poked out of the side of her mouth. Just like Ryann's did, thought Dan, amused. Then again, perhaps her engineering talents were running in his direction.

He looked at the revised drawing and noticed Mandy had shaped it like a rounded hovel. She definitely wanted more than shade, and was drawing fuzzy lines over the surface that resembled brush and reeds.

"It looks like an Indian house, Mandy."

"That's what it is!" She was obviously pleased that Dan had recognized her efforts. "Will you make it for me?"

"I'm not sure I know how to do it." Dan shivered involuntarily. "It's chilly in here! Is the window open?"

"Mamma opened it to make it warm."

Slouch was sleeping contentedly on his rug, and didn't pay any attention to Dan when he closed the window.

"Let me tell you a story now. Okay, Daddy?"

Dan returned to his place on Mandy's bed. "Okay, tell me your story."

In the patronizing tone that Mandy frequently used when talking to her dolls, she began.

"Once upon a time there were three bears. They lived in a little girl's room, and they kept her company while she was sick."

At least it wasn't the same old story, thought Dan.

Mandy's voice dropped to a whisper and she continued, "Then they came alive and began to talk to each other. But the little girl didn't know what they were saying!"

Mandy looked into her father's face with a mixed expression of panic and a plea for understanding. This was more than a bedtime story. She was testing his confidence in her. Dan knew his seven-year-old daughter. She was afraid. Something was going on and she was trying to find a way to tell him.

This was just how he imagined Mandy would have told him if a stranger had approached her. She would have carefully tested his acceptance, his ability to handle a situation, by telling him a fairy tale, which re-enacted the scene. Mandy was a child sensitive to the feelings of others. Even her dog, Dan thought.

"Do you think the little girl was sick and maybe imagined the bears talking?" Dan asked.

"No, Daddy," Mandy said regretfully. "The bears talk a different language."

Dan tried to deal with it directly. He explained to Mandy that a fever sometimes makes you *think* you are hearing things, or seeing things. This was called a hallucination, he said.

She looked at him sadly and sighed, "Yes, maybe it's a ha-lu-sa-shun."

Mandy said her head was beginning to hurt, and not wanting to press the issue, Dan checked the note pad for her schedule of medication. He encouraged her to make a last trip to the bathroom, and then Dan tucked her in bed.

***

The weather man said a large storm was on its way, and Ryann thought it was just as well they couldn't go anywhere. She didn't regret Dan taking their car to work. The near miss in Jack's car had frightened her. How fragile their lives had suddenly become. Life was walloping them from all sides right now, and Ryann felt an urgent need to be vigilant.

She and Dan had talked late into the night. They had finally shared their thoughts about Mandy. Tentatively, Dan had told her about the drawing and the bear story. He made no comment on Mandy's behavior, and waited to see what Ryann had to say. Ryann had finally asked, "What's going on, anyway?" Her eyes had brimmed with tears, as she faced the reality of her fears. As despondent as she had first felt, neither she nor Dan were alone any longer to try and make sense out of this craziness. It was so easy to be intimidated by Mandy's bizarre behavior. Ryann had told herself more than once that she was reading more into things than was warranted, but now they were openly discussing the possibility of Mandy's hallucinations being fever-induced. And they both discounted it.

They were Mandy's parents. They knew their daughter and were now considering some of her past remarks in a different light -- they had begun before the onset of Valley Fever, and were spoken with complete candor and in earnest innocence. Ryann couldn't dismiss the idea that something psychic might be going on. Was Mandy in touch with events going on in some other part of the world? Was their daughter experiencing E.S.P.? It was certainly eccentric behavior. Ryann could hardly deal with these thoughts, much less discuss them with anyone except Dan. After all, they were rational, civilized people who looked for answers in science, and questions that had no answers were best left to God.

The wind began to blow a little before noon, and Ryann went outside to make sure the patio furniture and trashcans were battened down. As she stepped out the door a strong gust took her breath away. Ryann turned her face and gasped. Chicago had prepared her for strong winds, but she hadn't expected them in Arizona.

Several aluminum chairs were strewn across the lawn, and the huge tamarack was thrashing above her head. Ryann quickly picked up and moved into the garage everything that wasn't tied down. Her hair had whipped around her face and she fought to see between flying locks as she made her way to the kitchen door.

Ryann opened the backdoor and it was flung from her hand. Slouch, who had been waiting for this moment, ran from the house and into the yard. His tail was between his legs and he was yelping as if someone was chasing him with intention to do bodily harm. There was nothing in the open doorway, and in the instant Ryann confirmed this Slouch ran across the yard and easily vaulted the fence.

It had all happened so fast Ryann hadn't time to even call his name. She closed the door, cutting off the howling wind behind her, and hurried to Mandy's bedroom. As she approached her daughter's room, she heard Mandy's voice. She was talking to someone. No, it sounded more like an argument.

"Mandy?" Ryann entered the room and immediately shivered. Mandy didn't acknowledge her presence, but continued addressing what Ryann believed were the bears, seated at the little red table. Her face was flushed and she yelled angrily, "How can I understand what you're saying when you don't speak English? I'm sick, can't you tell?"

Mandy's head fell back on the pillow. "You're 'pose to be nice to me!" she pleaded in a softer tone.

"Mandy!" Ryann said sharply. She had to bring her back from wherever she had gone. "Mandy, its okay. It's all right, baby." Ryann held her close, trying to protect her from something that frightened her even more than her daughter.

"Mommy?" She recognized Ryann at once and said firmly, "It's not all right, Mommy!"

Ryann watched her daughter grow sleepy and was relieved to see the subject closed. The room was freezing and she pulled the extra blankets close around Mandy. She wondered, who do you go to when stuff like this happens ... a psychiatrist?

***

Thursday only became worse. By late afternoon, Ryann was a nervous wreck. When Mandy was awake she was either having some imaginary argument, displaying a temper that

Ryann had never seen the likes of, or she was crying pitifully for her dog. There was no in between, except sleep.

When Mandy woke after the first episode, Ryann tried to get her to eat some soup. She thought it might warm her, being in the cold room. Mandy did not even recognize her, but she did plead for Slouch.

The afternoon wore on and when the doorbell rang Ryann thought it incongruous. She answered the door and found Lisa Owens standing on the porch, clutching Thad and Tracy as if the wind would blow them away. Ryann brought them into the living room and offered them a seat. There was none of the usual joviality, and the kids sat still and silent beside their mother. Ryann noticed Lisa's red, swollen eyes and gently asked what was wrong.

"Oh, Ryann," A storm of tears filled Lisa's eyes and she fought to control her emotions.

"I know you have your own problems right now, with Mandy sick and all, but I didn't know where to go on such short notice."

Ryann was beginning to understand that Lisa had left Jack, was intending to take the kids to her father's in Colorado, but needed temporary sanctuary. Lisa volunteered enough information about Jack's behavior to convince her to help.

"I'm really afraid for our lives," Lisa said, low enough not to be overheard by the children.

Dan wasn't the only one, thought Ryann.

There was a welcome interlude while Ryann went to find some of Mandy's toys with which the kids could play. When she came back she poured Lisa a glass of ice tea. Without elaboration, Ryann told her things weren't going so well in this house either. Mandy's scream interrupted their conversation, and Ryann, seemingly composed, offered Lisa the use of the phone to make plane reservations before she went to Mandy's room.

***

Mandy was hysterical. She was sitting, board straight, in the middle of the bed and screaming.

"I want Slouch! Bring him back to me! You've got to bring him back to me, Mommy!"

"Mandy, he's outside somewhere. He jumped the fence and I don't know where he is." Ryann tried hard to calm her daughter.

"He's looking for the bone. The bears made him do it, but I want him back. I'm scared of the bears, Mommy!" Mandy was speaking faster, and in panic it sounded like gibberish.

The fear was real and so were sounds of conspiracy and paranoia. Ryann was frantic. What could she do? She didn't have the car and she couldn't leave Mandy alone. And then she thought of Lisa. Maybe, Lisa wouldn't mind watching her for a little while.

When Ryann returned to the kitchen, Lisa was just hanging up the phone. There was a flight to Denver departing Phoenix at ten-fifteen this evening, Lisa informed her. Would she put up with them for just a couple of hours, she asked.

"Oh, yes! Lisa, now I must ask you a favor," Ryann knew the tone of her voice was much too desperate. She deliberately slowed down and made an attempt to calm herself.

"Mandy is delirious from the fever. The doctor said it's to be expected, but *please* will you watch Mandy while I look for her dog? He's running somewhere in the neighborhood. I know it will help quiet her to have Slouch back."

"Of course, why don't you use my car, Ryann?"

Ryann was hoping for this offer. Chasing Slouch was just a little much, under the circumstance.

***

Nothing was stranger than someone else's car. Ryann forced herself to concentrate on the instrument panel and when she was certain that once she began she would be able to complete the motions, she turned on the ignition. She felt her heart pound, and reached inside for a calmer place. Everyone had one, she was sure. Hers was an oasis in a storm, her inner self, where nothing could touch, or trouble, or confuse. Ryann had the car on the road, when she thought of Dan's drawing of the palm house. She wondered if it represented Dan's oasis.

She hadn't thought about where she was going when she tore out of the house, but she did now. Slouch was sure to have returned to the construction site. Mandy knew it, but more remarkably, Ryann did too. Slouch was after a bone and not just any bone. This had something to do with the experience on the day they visited the veterinarian.

The intersection of Devonshire and Vine was empty. School had been out for several hours, and traffic had slowed. Ryann turned on to Vine and looked ahead for the graded lot. She drove past the familiar houses and found her address. Nothing much had occurred in the way of construction. Equipment was abandoned. Probably, the end of a work day, she thought.

She looked ahead carefully, and sure enough there was Slouch, his wiry body more taut than usual. Ryann stopped the car and watched the dog. He was standing at the edge of the pit. With his hair on end and his exaggerated stiff limbs, he reminded Ryann of a cartoon dog she had seen struck by lightning. A car honking jolted her attention to the rear view mirror where she noticed a truck had pulled up behind her.

It was Jerod and he was waving wildly at her. Ryann got out of the car to join him.

"What happened? Your dog run away, again?" he asked, teasingly.

Ryann was startled by Jerod's appearance. He had a good start on a beard and she would have thought that was intentional, except for the rest of his appearance. The look on her face betrayed her appraisal, and Jerod smiled self-consciously.

He walked over to her. Searching her face, he said confidentially. "I've been going through some shit, if you don't mind the language. But, frankly, you don't look so hot, either."

She imagined he was right. Ryann evaluated her own wired state and thought it had to show.

"Mandy, my daughter, is sick," she said. "Her dog has run away and she's calling for him. I'm sure glad to find him here."

Slouch was standing at the hole's edge, intermittently barking and howling, as if struggling with an uncommitted challenge.

"Let me put him in the car before he has the neighbors complaining. But I must talk to you about your rash, if you've got a minute?"

"Sure. I just came down to check on the equipment." Jerod answered, and walked over with her to get the dog.

Ryann thought he must have taken off work. Maybe, by now he knew what was making him sick. She wondered how he would react to being told he might have Valley Fever.

The dog had overcome his fear and was in the pit digging furiously at the base of the bank. Slouch was growling and unaware of their approach.

"Hey, boy!" said Jerod, softly. "It's okay. That's my bear bone you're after, huh?"

"What did you say?" Ryann couldn't have heard right.

But Jerod didn't hear her. He got Slouch's attention finally and, with a hand on his collar, was encouraging him back up the bank.

***

"What did you mean back there about a bear bone?" Ryann asked.

"That's what I've been doing here lately, digging for bones ... fossils, actually," he corrected himself. "Also, it's why I'm such a mess. Crazy things have been happening to me since I found some rocks and a fossil of a prehistoric bear."

Jerod expected real skepticism from Ryann, but not what he was about to hear.

"Slouch is here for the same reason. That's what Mandy said and I believe her."

"The dog?"

"Uh huh," Ryann backed up and leaned against the car's fender. She felt like the wind had been knocked out of her.

"You better let me explain first. I've been meaning to find you, to tell you that Slouch has Valley Fever and Mandy, too."

She explained that the dog was diagnosed at the vet's the day they met. Ryann told him about the disease being caused by a fungus and that the fungus could live for years in western soil.

"That's why Slouch coughed, because it's in his lungs. But Mandy has it, too. Humans with Valley Fever usually have a rash." Ryann looked down at Jerod's hands, and then continued.

"Fever and delirium are other symptoms." Her eyes questioned his, begging to know if she should continue.

"Go on." There was no turning back. Jerod couldn't stop this revelation if he'd wanted.

Ryann's voice quivered. "Mandy is hallucinating, or Dan and I *think* she is hallucinating. She says that bears are talking, but she can't understand what they're saying. And what's worse, I think the dog hears them, too!"

"I understand."

"Do you? Do you really know what we're going through? Oh, I know I must sound crazy." She was almost to the point of tears.

Jerod remembered his impulsive need to break away from reading, to come down here today, and at this particular time. Was it just luck that he ran into Ryann? He knew what Ryann must be going through. To live through this fear for her daughter had to be worse than even Jerod's experience.

"You're not going crazy, Ryann. And neither is Mandy. I've had some kind of hallucination or psychic experience, too. I know it's hard to believe, but there is some connection between what your daughter is telling you and what I know." He was still afraid to say too much. Jerod needed time to think. He needed to talk to Bill Martinez.

"There is someone I'm supposed to see tomorrow, someone I believe can help. Do you think that I can come over and talk to you and your husband tomorrow night, afterward? It's very important."

Ryann hadn't realized how alone with her thoughts she had been. She believed Jerod. Why would anyone make this up?

She opened the car door slightly, just enough to pull out her purse. Ryann fumbled for her checkbook and tore out a deposit slip with their imprinted name, address, and phone number.

"Here. Please, I will ... we will be expecting you," she corrected her self. "I've got to get back. Someone is watching Mandy and ..." Tears were blinding her and she turned away.

"I'll be there. I promise," Jerod said.

***

Chapter 13

ON THE EDGE

ON THE EDGE

Towering thunderheads hung above the desert like a foreboding kingdom. They made Ryann think of the great halls of mystical kings. The Arizona sky, usually two-dimensional, had opened its heavens, offering three-dimensional slate-black depths that half-hid its secret source of light rays. This panorama moved slowly into the valley like a giant set rolling onto a theater stage.

Ryann parked Lisa's car in the driveway and hurried to the house with Slouch. She felt the unsettled wind blow warm and cool about her legs. A storm was on its way, for sure.

"Lisa, do you think you'll be all right driving to Phoenix?" Ryann was genuinely concerned. Her world wasn't the only one in jeopardy, and she felt humbled by her own self-centeredness.

"I was just listening to the news. The storm isn't supposed to arrive until tomorrow afternoon. I suppose I should get under way soon, because there's a high-wind warning. Don't worry, I'll drive carefully."

Lisa's wan smile was an effort. Ryann wondered if Mandy had added to Lisa's troubles while she had been out looking for the dog. It didn't seem a good idea to volunteer an explanation. Who would believe it, anyway?

Slouch had gone to his water bowl in the kitchen. On his return to the living room he rebuffed the kids' attempt at play and headed straight for Mandy's room.

"Why don't you have dinner with us first, Lisa? Dan will be home any minute." She knew she was putting off her own problems, but there didn't seem to be an immediate alternative.

***

Thad and Tracy were planted in front of the TV watching cartoons. Ryann had to admit she was thankful for this electronic baby sitter. Lisa had fallen quiet with her own thoughts, and they both went through the automatic motions of preparing dinner and setting the table.

Dan came home, and though he was initially surprised to see Lisa and the kids, when she announced her decision to leave Jack, he didn't press for information.

They sat quietly at the large kitchen table, and Ryann explained that she would take a tray in to Mandy when she woke. Thad and Tracy looked with suspicion at their mother, who deliberately spooned a serving of broccoli onto each of their plates.

Tracy protested with her usual whining, a practice that exasperated her parents so that, in the past, they had caved in easily to her wants. Lisa ignored her for several minutes, and then unexpectedly reached out and grabbed her daughter's collar, turning Tracy toward her.

"You are going to eat your dinner, all of it, without another sound. Do you understand?" Lisa demanded.

"Yes." Tracy was stunned into submission. The shock value of this first undisputed order out of her mother's mouth had snapped her to attention. Faces around the table revealed that they, too, were impressed. There was no more conversation as they ate their dinner.

Ryann was thinking of all she had to discuss with Dan. She would be relieved when Lisa and the kids were gone. The need for privacy had never been so important to their marriage.

Mandy's voice suddenly broke the silence. She was urgently calling someone, but who?

Dan and Ryann rose from the table at the same time and neither protested the accompaniment of the other. As they made their way down the hallway they heard Mandy clearly call out "Golthlay!"

***

Jerod's first reaction had been to call Bill Martinez. It was really tempting to just dump it on the medicine man. He had already told him enough of what was going on yesterday when he called. Would he be shocked by anything new? Jerod dialed the number given him so long ago at the restaurant. Was it really just last Thursday? But the line was busy, and once again he was left to sort out things alone.

This thing about Valley Fever, it helped connect if not answer certain questions. On the coffee table Jerod found the list he had made earlier. He picked up the list and read number three, "coughing disease". Could it be Valley Fever? He checked the others and read number ten, "the rash".

Yes, this could be a common denominator. He had to find out more about Valley Fever. Jerod couldn't understand why he went back to Pete's bookshelf, except that he had found everything else there.

This time he seemed out of luck. This was not a medical library. Pete's interests were in archaeology, paleontology, and the Native Americans of the Southwest, not in real or imagined illnesses. Jerod realized he might have to go to the library or maybe talk to a doctor. If his own rash was caused by Valley Fever, that might be reason enough.

The phone rang and again forgetting why he had turned on the message recorder, Jerod reached for the receiver.

"Jerod! Where've you been? Don't you know you're supposed to play back your messages?" It was Pete and he didn't sound all that upset.

"Did you call? Oh, jeez." Jerod looked down at the flashing light on the machine. "I'm sorry, Pete!" Jerod was about to explain he had been busy, but he couldn't swallow that one himself.

"Never mind, its nothing urgent, I just wanted to let you know we'll be back on Saturday. A few side trips have delayed us, but on the whole it's been a profitable hunt."

Jerod was embarrassed. To be honest, he hadn't even thought of Pete or Jenny. Under the circumstances, he was doing what he could, right? Then focusing on his "circumstances" he impulsively asked, "Pete, would you know anything about a disease called Valley Fever?"

"Yeah. Why, do you have it?"

"Maybe. I've had a rash and a few other problems." It wouldn't be a good idea to parade his flights of fantasy in front of Pete's nose. He had a pretty good idea Pete already thought his future brother-in-law was working with less than a full deck.

"You can't do what I do, digging in the dirt, and not hear about Coccidioidomycosis, or Valley Fever, eventually. I'm surprised you haven't heard of it before. You run a risk, as well."

"I've been lucky I guess," Pete said. "I never caught it, but I've known many who have. Jerod, if you want to know more about it, there's an old Merck Manual somewhere in the house.

There are two actually. One is on veterinary medicine, but the other is on human illness.

"I picked up the books at a swap meet a few years back when I was concerned about tuberculosis ... another nasty thing endemic to our area. Natives had a low resistance to T.B. and many died as a result."

"Are you saying that T.B. can be mistaken for Valley Fever?" Jerod was genuinely alarmed.

"Naw! Not with today's medicine. But back around the turn of the century, I'm sure there was some confusion, because of similar symptoms like fever, cough, and chest pain. Then there is Blastomycosis, another fungal disease with some of the same symptoms, but different locale."

Jerod was not feeling so good. Pete had marvelous powers of suggestion. Before he hung up, Pete added that he was surprised to find the disease listed in the veterinary manual, too.

"Yes, I just found out an Airedale friend of mine has it," Jerod told him.

***

The alarm went off, and Jack opened his eyes to a hangover. He thought it strange about alcohol. You couldn't really sleep it off. If you didn't pay now you paid later, and this was later. The fuzzy thud of a headache was just beginning to emerge from hibernation. Jack knew what to expect when his feet hit the floor so he planned his next moves economically.

He took several aspirin from the bottle next to the bed and swallowed them with last night's beer. He wouldn't move until they began to work. Instead he thought about Lisa and the kids.

They weren't here, that's for sure. Jack guessed they probably went to Dan and Ryann's house. But she'd be back later, when she thought he'd been made to suffer enough. Well, the only suffering he would feel would be this damn hangover! Jack felt his anger begin to roust the beast in his head.

It was inevitable. He had to get up and go to work. Jack labored his way through a shower and made his way to the kitchen for a glass of orange juice. It dawned on him this was Friday. Son of a bitch! He still hadn't heard from the bank! He'd have to call the bank from work. The loan had to come through, and he'd go crazy not knowing the outcome until Monday.

Right now, the most important thing was to show up at work. If he played it cool, with his seniority, the layoff wouldn't affect him. Dan would get the axe instead ... too bad, really. He had nothing against Dan personally, though there was a kind of sweet justice, when he thought about it. Dan was meddling where he didn't belong, because Jack was positive, now that he was up and functioning, that Lisa and the kids were at the Thearles' house.

Mercifully the air was cool. The heat wave had broken under the dark Arizona sky. There was every indication that the storm coming was going to be a big one.

Jack stopped at a store on the way to work and bought a cup of coffee. He fumbled in his pocket for change and felt the special miniature camera he had put there earlier. The clerk stared knowingly at his shaking hand, and Jack had a sudden, vicious urge to throw the scalding coffee into those judgmental eyes.

He had reason, Jack wanted to yell. And in his head he felt the screams of emotions no longer held in check. He had to get hold of himself. This was going to be a crucial day in the life of Jack Owens. Don't blow it now, he thought, and then when several teenagers in the parking lot began to giggle, he realized he had been talking out loud.

There was a lot to do today, and the least of it was to work for Sin Par Space Technology. The empty feeling that had briefly settled on Jack when he thought of Lisa leaving was swamped by fears she would take him to the cleaners when she left. Or finish taking him to the cleaners, he cynically reminded himself. He had to protect his assets, whatever was left.

When the bank opened he would call and transfer the balance of their mutual accounts to the new account he'd opened in his own name last week. Though Jack was relatively certain their credit cards were all at their limits and flagged by the banks, he'd call this morning and state for the record he was no longer responsible. His head was swimming, and he didn't hear the "Good morning" of a fellow co-worker.

Jack focused on becoming as inconspicuous as possible. He walked purposely through the Engineering department to his work area, offering brusque greetings along the way, in hopes of discouraging any further conversation. His attitude said he was busy and not to be bothered, and the other engineers, long accustomed to his erratic moods, were happy enough to give him a wide berth.

Dan was actually relieved. There was enough on his own mind, without dealing with Jack's hurt feelings about the new driving arrangements. But that wasn't all, of course. Lisa and the kids had been at their house for several hours last night before they departed for the airport in Phoenix, and Dan was certain Jack would have called or confronted him here at work. After all, the Owens didn't have that many friends Lisa could go to for help.

Looking at him now through the glass top half of the cubicle partition, Dan thought Jack didn't really give a damn. He already seemed to be absorbed with his work.

***

Jack's terminal was on, but Jack was busy with other things. He made his series of planned calls the moment the financial world was open for business, and as the morning went on his panic increased. The reality of bankruptcy and a failed marriage was flashing in his mind as crazily as the screen before him. He willed himself to focus on the charade as long as he could, but it was all he could do to stay seated.

Three times that morning Jack called Grand West, and asked for Linda Caulfield's extension. Once the line disconnected, another time she was in a meeting, and the last time he was put through to the wrong department. Jack had found his self screaming into the phone, and was suddenly aware of the attention he'd drawn from the engineers around him. The person on the other end had hung up on him.

His mind started to wander in the manner it had, of late. Jack checked this means of escape and concentrated on solutions, the real ones. He knew the value of the work they were doing. There was a black market that would pay handsomely for work already approved, but not yet funded or in production. Several well-placed inquiries could connect him with these sources, he was sure. Hell, he had been approached before.

Jack supposed his willingness not to expose this contact at the time had everything to do with his wanting an ace up his sleeve. This looked like the time to call in the aces.

As an engineer, Jack was cleared for access to the CAD operations room, and he remembered that blueprints were being run off this morning of a highly classified project. A photograph of vellum, placed in the right hands, would solve all his financial problems, now and into the future.

Jack bided his time until lunch. There was no designated hour for lunch, but most of the guys ate together in the cafeteria. The CAD room usually emptied first, with the engineers leaving an hour later.

At nine minutes past twelve Jack got up from his chair and went into the hallway to find the bathroom. No one paid any attention to his leaving, except Dan. But Dan noted the time Jack left and the time he returned. It was twelve-thirty-two, twenty-three minutes later, and Dan thought this strange. Still, when he returned, Jack asked Dan if he would like to go eat. Apparently he'd been forgiven for driving to work alone.

"I could go for a bowl of clam chowder!" There was little on the cafeteria menu that Dan really liked, but Friday's soup was one of them.

Once seated in the cafeteria, Dan read the strained lines on Jack's face. He'd suffered since Lisa left, and there was no way Dan could just ignore it.

"Are you managing all right?"

Jack's eyes jerked up from his plate, and Dan thought they looked like those of a wounded animal.

"If you're referring to Lisa's leaving -- good riddance!" Jack hissed.

There was such immediate vehemence in Jack's reply. Dan wondered just how close he was to the edge.

***

The afternoon was unbearable for Jack. He had set a goal for himself, to cover as many bases as possible. The brief respite for lunch was a meager gesture of sympathy directed to Dan. This was sure to be his last day, and Jack could afford the gratuity. The axe always fell on Friday, and Dan, having least seniority, would be laid off today.

Jack managed to call and placate a few creditors, but he felt foolishly conspicuous and exposed. It was a tightrope walk, making the calls necessary for survival and feigning work at the same time. His ace-in-the-hole had been played and lost.

He had managed to enter the CAD room undetected from the hallway, no problem. But he had not considered the security precautions that would be taken when everyone in the room was at lunch. Jack looked everywhere and finally concluded the blueprints were under lock and key. The irony was he could not use his legitimate clearance access without bringing attention to himself. He knew this was not the time to risk it. Maybe Monday, he thought.

The cool Engineering Department, with its dimmed lights, that further emphasized a shaded environment, did little to cool Jack. He was perspiring heavily, and his shirt stuck to his back each time he leaned forward in his swivel chair.

At four-thirty Jack got through to Phoenix and the inept phone maze to Linda's desk. He breathed a sigh of relief only to have his hopes dashed when a voice he didn't recognize answered.

"This is Pam Sitka. May I help you?"

"Is Linda there?" Jack asked, impatiently.

"Jerod! Is that you?" And before Jack could correct her, she continued excitedly. "If you're in Tucson, stay put. Linda left early for her brother's house in Tucson.

"So how are you doing?" she continued. "Haven't seen you in quite a while," she added, obviously prepared to chat awhile.

"Fine." Jack didn't offer any more. He was curious. So, the bitch was on her way here. Maybe they would connect, if he allowed this blithering idiot, Pam, to continue volunteering information.

"God, I'm glad to hear it! Linda was really worried when she called Pete's house and got the message you recorded, but she should be there in an hour or so."

Jack disengaged himself from this one-sided conversation as smoothly as possible. He put the receiver gently on its cradle and thought over what he had just learned.

Linda Caulfield would be in Tucson within an hour. She would be going to her brother's house, Pete ... Caulfield, who else? Most likely there was a directory listing for a Pete Caulfield in Tucson. He could look that up and get an address. And he could go there and confront her, damn it!

He had to know about the loan. Jack knew he simply could not get through this weekend without an answer. And what if it was the wrong answer? Linda Caulfield had the power to make or break him. But maybe, just maybe, Jack could give her a few lessons of his own.

As Jack sat there and thought about what he was going to do, he began to feel more in control. This frenetic day, with everyone messing with him, was almost finished. He would be calling the shots once again. Jack Owens was back in town!

There was one thing, he was curious about. What was the deal about the "message" that had worried Linda? Jack was not one to miss a trick. Maybe this twit, Pam, had inadvertently given him the final weapon. Jack reached down to the bottom shelf beside his chair and pulled out the Tucson directory. There was only one listing for a Peter Caulfield. This had to be it.

He dialed the number and let it ring until he heard the click of the recorder.

"Linda. I'm sorry I missed you, babe. I think I'm starting to put this all together. In any case, I've got to follow through. If you need to reach me, I'll be at the Thearle residence, 1341 Devonshire in Tucson. Their phone number is 395-2713. Love you!"

Jack wasn't sure he heard correctly. He scrambled to copy the message, fumbling for a piece of paper, and after the beep, which indicated he was to leave a message, he dropped the receiver like a hot potato. The Thearle residence! What in the hell? And now Jack's mind began to stretch and expand like a worn balloon giving in warped and weakened areas. He could actually feel the bulges of pressure build. He had to get out of here. He had to make sense of this. He had to.

It was closing time, mercifully. Lester Gaines was standing in front of Jack's chair and Jack wasn't sure how long he had been standing there. He had an envelope in his hand and he was offering it to Jack. The old coot had been talking, but Jack couldn't make any sense out of his words. He decided it best to just agree and accept the envelope. The sooner he did, the sooner he could leave. Jack desperately needed to get away.

***

Chapter 14

A STATE OF MIND

A STATE OF MIND

Friday morning Jerod woke to the sound of rain on the flat roof. He was surprised to find that he had slept through the night without a nightmare or a trip somewhere. He stretched lazily and listened to the drumming rain, a reassuring sound considering the relentless wind that had blown all yesterday. For the first time in a long while Jerod thought about his future.

Jerod envisioned a time beyond events now occurring, when Linda and he could make their relationship permanent. In his imagination, from this point he could look back curiously on how he had misspent his energies fighting contrived demons. Was it as easy as adopting a different state of mind? Was maturity nothing more than learning to trust and accept your self?

It sounded so boring from the standpoint of youth. But more tolerable now, Jerod thought. Would he really possess the wisdom that could ... would ... eventually come with age? He only knew that now, for the first time, he was beginning to feel peace. He couldn't say he was satisfied with all that he had learned lately, but there was a real triumph in the reasoning process, and there was the knowledge that in bringing order out of chaos he had reason to expect it might be repeated throughout the universe.

If this was a path he was traversing, or some sort of spiritual journey, he knew he belonged here as assuredly as the rain on the roof. At first Jerod had wanted no part of it ... he'd felt victimized. But he knew that somehow his own growth was dependent on a certain vulnerability, and now he was committed to exploring it. No wonder he imagined a commitment to Linda.

When Jerod thought about the twenty-odd years since Vietnam he saw his self frozen in a time warp for a good part of it. In those earlier days he functioned without purpose. He wasn't in charge, maybe nobody was. In fact, when he met Linda didn't she tell him this was what was wrong with him? He couldn't look ahead, wouldn't plan ahead. Instead he confronted her fiercely, defending his preoccupation with the present. "We might not live to see tomorrow," had been his excuse.

He knew now he'd actually hoped he wouldn't. There hadn't been any reason to plan for a tomorrow you didn't want to face. Life had been shit for too long, and he had lived a death wish. When Linda came into his life, he was introduced to her perspective, but it had taken a hallucination to have one his self.

***

Jerod felt a mounting excitement as the morning progressed. Places to go and people to see, or so goes the saying. He smiled. There was an emerging itinerary, in spite of his disorganization.

He looked down at his hands. The rash was almost gone, but there were several lesions that looked open and raw, as well as a few more on his face. Jerod thought that the biggest problem might be the danger of infection. He probably should see a doctor, he told himself, but somehow he didn't believe the medical profession would have a clue as to what was happening to him. Not like Bill did, anyway.

A lot had happened since he talked to Bill on the phone on Wednesday, but it helped to know Bill had most of the story and enough pertinent background and genuine interest. Jerod had told him about the trip to the mountain, about meeting the Native man and the sick child, even about Pete's identifying the fossil as *Arctodus* bear. Though there was much Jerod didn't understand about the supposed powers of a medicine man, he had implicit trust in this man, and he trusted his own ability to distinguish sincerity from sham. He did have a partner in this adventure, or maybe Bill was more like a guide.

His main purpose this afternoon was to meet with Bill, but Jerod found he was also looking forward to the AA meeting. There was strength in this group of men, and comfort.

The rain had washed the air and a clean earthen smell came through the doorway. Jerod opened the sliding glass door to the patio, and standing in the entrance inhaled deep lungs' full of the freshened air. He was amazed how this cleared his mind in such an effortless way.

It was easy to face cleaning the cluttered house. Pete and Jenny would be back tomorrow and Jerod thought he'd better show his responsible side before they returned. For the next couple of hours he became a whirlwind houseboy. Jerod's energy was high and to feed his enthusiasm he thought to turn on the stereo. He went through Pete and Jenny's compact disc collection, uncertain what would suit his mood. He pulled out the "Grand Canyon Suite", by Ferda Grofe, and intrigued by the title, decided to listen to it while he worked.

He began cleaning and picking up things around the house. As he worked he fell under the spell of the music's visual theme, which repeated the sounds of falling rain. Jerod's mood was becoming too large to contain. In this expansive frame of mind he felt the melodies reach inside to fill his soul and body, then the house, and finally, flow outside. It was a powerful, rejuvenating experience, unfamiliar until now. Eventually, he had to face the competing noise of the vacuum cleaner, but he hurried through this chore, and started the disc over from the beginning. These were new levels of feelings Jerod had never before explored, exhilarating emotions, and he wasn't drugged or drunk, he reminded himself.

Jerod thought about his promise to Ryann to see her and her husband tonight, and remembered it was Friday and Linda might decide to drive down. He decided to leave a message on the recorder, letting her know where he'd gone, in case she called. Jerod gave some hint of the urgency, but after he recorded his message, he wondered if he should explain more in a note.

"Don't worry," he added on paper. "I'll be seeing Bill Martinez first. I think this man is the only one who can help. I may be late." He signed it, "Love ya, Jerod". As an afterthought, but one with much previous consideration, he wrote, "P.S. Pete and Jenny called and said they would be in tomorrow. Do you think that would be a good time to announce our engagement?"

***

Canal Road was washed out in places. Jerod gripped the steering wheel and tried to concentrate on avoiding the many potholes through the sheet of rain falling on the windshield. The storm was taking a bigger toll out here. Or, city hall just didn't care as much about the condition of roads leading to a poorer part of town.

Jerod looked at the clock on the dash, ten minutes till two. He wondered if anyone would show up at the old church for the AA meeting. It was downright nasty, and he thought his meeting with Bill the only reason good enough for him to come out on a day like this.

There were four old cars in the parking lot besides Bill's blue truck. Never underestimate man's desire for sobriety, Jerod reminded himself. It was encouraging to know other men would push for their own survival. Jerod pulled in beside Bill's pickup. He felt like he'd just returned home.

The universality of Alcoholic Anonymous' brotherhood impressed Jerod again, as it had each time he attended a meeting. This family, forged from the same pain, had a stronger tie than blood. It was the only family many of these men had; the wives, parents, and children ... another group of casualties ... left abandoned in the wake of alcohol's destruction. Here the men felt acceptance. Some never progressed beyond this point, but they all felt the fellowship, and recognized this as the place of possibilities.

Jerod's eyes fell on Bill Martinez as soon as he entered the community room. Bill acknowledged his presence, and their covenant, with a gentle nod of his head. Jerod felt his quiet reassurance as he took a folding chair and joined the circle.

The meeting would be short in comparison to others, but one of those especially intense meetings, which inspired each man to leave markedly strengthened. There were four men besides Bill and Jerod, and each of the men spoke, in turn, from a deep need to articulate feelings.

Tentatively, a worn and beaten man, Jerod guessed to be in his thirties, rose from his chair. He fumbled with a pack of cigarettes, gave his name as Gary, and said he was an alcoholic. He stood quietly, obviously troubled by the inner effort required to speak. Then cautiously he began and from the boldness of this first step, apparently drew power.

From such beginnings he, and others around the table, found their way to the crossroads of enlightenment. As each spoke in humble honesty he crossed a threshold, entering a land of personal discoveries, where those encircling him bore witness.

Through the open doors Jerod watched the gentle rain splashing on the walkway, and wondered if he had anything to offer. His journey, his crossroads weren't of this world. How could he speak of another place, another time? What did he know that he hadn't known before? What had he brought back that he could share? As he stood, he felt Bill's eyes on him like a blessing.

"There is a future," he began. "I feel it's important to tell you this, because you may doubt it. I know I did.

"The Big Book talks of spiritual awareness. In there you've read about the importance of finding your relationship to your Higher Power. This always bothered me. It was as if there was a secret inner circle, one where I didn't belong, because I hadn't had the spiritual experience every one talked about.

"I went through the motions. I've read the Big Book. I read the Bible, but nothing happened, no matter how I pushed for it to happen. I don't know all the reasons for that, but I know now I was looking for someone else's experience. I had this preconceived idea of how truth would reveal itself to me, and I think I was trying to create or design my own spiritual experience.

"In my state of mind I was preventing it from happening. I'd closed the door to my own future. But I want to tell you something. There has to be a power greater than myself, because I was shown! I was taken there, yelling and kicking, against my will, to a place where I was made to see and made to listen.

"I'm back now, and I want to learn about this other state of mind. The one where I am the student and my Higher Power is the teacher."

The room was silent. Each man felt the reverberation of Jerod's words, deep inside where it touched something within, connecting in its own way, one soul to another. Jerod recalled the words from the Bible, "where two or more are gathered ..." and he knew the joy that grew from this power.

Bill rose from his chair and smiled benevolently on Jerod. The men remained frozen in respect for this moment. Then the medicine man closed the meeting.

"We must imagine a better world, before we can make one. We see it when we allow our Higher Power to create it within us. This is the way out of alcoholism. This is the way out of despair."

Bill Martinez spoke softly, pausing after each sentence, and every man was lifted with his words.

***

The conclave ended, and the men went out into the rain to find their cars. To find their way, thought Jerod.

He and Bill agreed to take Jerod's truck and return to the coffee shop where they had first met. Jerod reached behind the seat and felt reassuringly for the bundle. He grasped it and handed it to Bill who put it on his lap without comment.

While they drove the rain fell quietly from a dark sky. Jerod would have thought the scene melancholy, except he would have had to deny his own joy and that was impossible. It was hard to contain his excitement.

"Why don't you open it now, Bill?" Jerod was anxious to know. Bill untied the sleeves of the shirt and carefully examined its contents. He placed his weathered hands on the fossil and closed his eyes. Jerod fought his own curiosity, and kept his eyes glued to the road. The minutes passed in silence while Jerod parked the truck in front of the restaurant.

"This is my power stone," Bill said simply, and when he turned to look at Jerod his dark eyes were glistening.

"Because I was born and I will die one day, I am the beginning and I am the end," he continued. "And while I am here, on this our Mother Earth, I am the creator.

"This is only another way of saying we are all part of the Creator, and we will be known by our works. But my works, Jerod, are now possible because you have brought me the bone of Grandfather Bear."

Bill was preparing to retie the bundle when Jerod said, "Why don't you put the fossil in your pocket instead?"

Bill drew out an old leather pouch from inside his Levi jacket and removed a small piece of material. He carefully wrapped the bear fossil and placed it in his pouch.

They entered the restaurant and found their same table, out of the way of traffic. Jerod ordered coffee and immediately returned to their conversation.

"When you and I talked on the phone, and I told you what Pete had said about the fossil being that of *Arctodus* bear, I knew it too. I knew, somehow, the fossil's rightful place was with you.

"It doesn't answer any questions for me, though. Not personally. Not about the rock that spoke to me, or this communication with Golthlay, or Geronimo as you say his name is in English." Jerod knew his frustration was inappropriately abrasive. "I'm sorry Bill. I'm not as patient as I want to be," he admitted.

Bill was quiet for a time, his eyes focused on some imagined distance.

"Let me see if I can explain. Back there at the meeting you referred to your hallucination as a spiritual experience, your spiritual experience. You were right, of course.

"Those things which physically set apart one religion from another, one people from another, one way of reaching God from another way, are ultimately irrelevant. God determines the style of our spiritual experience. It is like language. Would we understand words of truth if they were not spoken in a language we understood?

"Generally, no, but perhaps God decides a message requires a particular messenger, one who does not necessarily understand the language, but can be counted on to deliver it."

"Bill! That's it!" Jerod felt a rush of recognition. He knew he had just seen a marker along the way, a sign that confirmed he was, indeed, on the right road.

"There is something else that happened -- was it yesterday? I can't believe it was just yesterday. Yes, Thursday," he assured himself aloud.

"I drove back over to the job to check on a few things. The woman who was looking for her dog was there. Ryann Thearle is her name. I guess the dog got away again and headed straight back to the site where I found the fossil.

"Anyway, Ryann was very upset. Her daughter Mandy was sick and was hallucinating. Their dog was sick, too, and they both had Valley Fever. The way, in which she described the disease, it could be what Golthlay's Yellow Bird was experiencing. Maybe, what his people were dying from. Hell, it could even be what I have."

"Tell me about the disease," Bill said.

"Well, Ryann told me a little about Valley Fever, but I looked it up in a Merck Manual when I returned home. The medical term is Coccidioidomycosis and it has other common names in the Southwest. The thing is it's a fungus that lives in the earth and has probably been here for centuries.

"The symptoms, according to what I've read, can include rash, fever, or influenza-like symptoms. The book said treatment is not needed for this primary pulmonary disease. Many people are asymptomatic and don't even know they have it!

"But the progressive type may develop from the primary disease. Dissemination may take place a few weeks, months, or even years later and involve the bones, joints, internal organs, or even the brain, which can be affected with meningitis. The progressive type is fatal in 55 to 60 percent of cases.

"What do you think? Do you see a connection?"

"There may be." Bill pondered the symptoms Jerod gave. "You know there is a connection that defies time.

"Man has become so estranged from earth and nature that the harmful consequences are duplicated on many levels. The sun that once nourished and revitalized our world within a harmony of perfection is now harmful to all life. And now we cannot look on the face of God. The shame is too much. The pain is the Earth's pain, our pain. It is the same.

"When you begin to grasp this, you learn that behind all illness, all disease, there is cause -- an accumulative transgression that has reaped an ecological doom.

"The very earth that gave us life has been offended and now makes us ill. A hundred years makes no difference in eternity. Because we are not alone, though we sometimes think so, perhaps Mandy's pain is Yellow Bird's pain."

Jerod could see the sense of this. It was true on a level that surpassed his intellect, and yet did not contradict it.

The waitress came to their table to refill their coffee cups. Bill covered his cup with his hand and said, "No more, thank you." When she left, Jerod noticed Bill hadn't touched the first cup.

"Is there something wrong with it?" Jerod asked.

"No. I mustn't drink coffee now. I'll explain later.

"What you have told me about your hallucination, as you call it, could be a parallel world. Certain events have happened. Could the outcome of the past be altered by a course of action today?" Bill smiled and Jerod once more felt his benediction.

"Or in your case, Jerod, could today's events be influenced by an intervention in the past? Remember what I said earlier? *We must imagine a better world before we can make one.*

"Sometimes a hallucination substitutes for a lack of imagination. It may take you out of a time warp temporarily, long enough to become inspired, motivated, and in control."

The pieces were coming together with tremendous speed. Jerod remembered the "rushing" he'd experienced when he moved from the present to the past, and thought it was nothing compared to this. That had been physical and this is mental, he thought. He had just picked up and moved to another state of mind. It had happened so fast he hadn't brought any excess baggage.

"Are you telling me that I can help Mandy?"

"I'm reminding you that you were asked to intervene," said Bill. "The first time we met you told me the masked dancer said, 'I call on you, Great Spirit. Intervene!' Remember?

"From what you've read, you now know he was the Gan dancer, the Black One, who spoke to you. He addressed you as Great Spirit and perhaps you are his spirit.

"And when you went to the mountain, didn't Golthlay call you the Great White Spirit, and ask you to stay with the child until the Holy Man returned?"

Jerod thought Bill hadn't missed anything. He had been putting together pieces of the puzzle, as well.

"There is something else. I believe Golthlay is the Black One. We know they are both concerned with helping the child. They were both part of the Medicine Spirit Dance. The Black One failed to keep all harm away during the ceremony. I don't know why. There could be other reasons, I suppose, but if someone identified the Black One and called out his real name, Golthlay, harm would *not* be kept away.

"The Holy Man has gone to the Mountain People to seek their power directly, so we know the Medicine Spirit Dance did not enlist their support. The proof is Yellow Bird and maybe others are sick.

"Yes, Jerod, you were asked to help. And now, I too, have been asked to help. We must ask Usen, the Creator, the Ruler, the Supreme Being to help us."

Jerod supposed he had already known the objective, subconsciously. The trip to the mountain was to serve a purpose greater than his. Jerod guessed he'd better get on with it, but the thought that followed this one was humbling.

"How?" Jerod asked.

"That's my line." Bill answered, with just a hint of a smile.

***

Chapter 15

INTERVENTION

INTERVENTION

"You know, I can just imagine the reaction of Mandy's parents. Well, maybe not Ryann. I can still see the look on her face at the job site. She's been shaken as badly as I have been. I'm sure she is considering things she never would have believed before her daughter's illness. But her husband, I don't know what kind of man is he. How is he taking all of this?"

"I don't know," Bill answered honestly. "But I believe you're going to have to find out. There is no way we can help either child without being with them. Didn't you say Golthlay asked you to stay and help Yellow Bird until the Holy Man returned?

"This will only begin to make sense when you see the duplicative aspect of this parallel world. If we are to help Yellow Bird, we must help Mandy. And in this other place and time, who is with Yellow Bird now?" Bill asked.

"Golthlay! Are you saying I'm Golthlay? Geronimo?"

"Jerod, I can't give you answers to questions like these. It is presumptuous for one man to interpret another man's truth. You may find that the answer to this question may be irrelevant, or you may find it is true." There was a deep sadness in Bill's voice.

"My role is to shed light on your path by helping you to interpret the dream. In this sense I am the counterpart to Golthlay's Holy Man. This is not all I am here to do. For in the light of Usen is truth *and* healing, Mandy's healing.

"You are to prepare the way; to talk with her parents and help them understand; to stay and comfort the child while I prepare for the intervention." Bill raised his hand, anticipating Jerod's next question.

"Think of what you know about the word intervention -- to interfere with the affairs of others. An intervention is a confrontation, in effect a hostile act. Not necessarily one to be received with open arms. Rather the opposite of conversion, huh? Most people convert by adopting or changing from one belief, religion, doctrine, or opinion to another.

"A conversion is a left-brain act, it's achieved by way of integrated logic. Usually, it is a nice and quiet thinking process, acceptable because it was fed through our senses in orderly fashion.

"However, sometimes, as you have learned, Jerod, truth comes in a blinding flash of light, circumventing a lack of imagination. Some of my people have sought this path or more correctly, to be put on "the path" by using peyote. It is a decision with heavy responsibility, because once a man has been put on the path he must be ready to follow it.

"You are familiar, I'm sure, with the many lost souls that had hoped a mind-altering drug would reveal truth, bringing them instant knowledge and happiness. There are ultimately no shortcuts, Jerod. We can only use what we are ready to receive. We mortals of this material world have craved a quick fix to all of our problems and the earth's. And as a result we have become junkies and alcoholics, addicted to the idea of instant gratification.

"The spiritual path of revelation is a window of opportunity. That is all. And yours has been made possible with Valley Fever."

***

Jerod was stunned. In silence he tried to absorb all that Bill was saying. His questions were being answered faster than he could think them. Focusing on the table in front of them, Jerod asked the only question Bill had not anticipated.

"You haven't answered me. Why aren't you drinking coffee?"

"I, too, have a pilgrimage to make. I must purify my mind and my body." Bill finished his glass of water, and in a tone which implied an ending and a beginning, said, "We've got work to do."

They agreed that Jerod would leave for the Thearles' home, and Bill would come in several hours when he was prepared. Jerod wrote out the address and directions on his napkin and handed it solemnly across the table.

Bill rose to his feet and several patrons looked over to their table. Already Jerod had taken for granted the majesty of this man. He was more than a curiosity to him, more than a Native with chiseled features and silver braids. He was a holy man, he was a shaman, and Jerod's guide.

At the cash register people were entering through the restaurant's double doors. Wind and rain whipped in the open doorway, and Jerod could see and feel the storm waiting to envelope him and Bill.

***

It was seven-thirty when Jerod stopped at a phone booth, and called to let the Thearles know he was on his way. Ryann had answered the phone and said somewhat cynically that they were looking forward to seeing him. Jerod knew this would be a long night, as it had been a long day. The innocence of the morning, the joyous anticipation he had known had grown old, and Jerod felt like Methuselah.

The rain was coming down in sheets. Flash flood conditions, thought Jerod. Desert storms were like that. Drought and heat would plague the Arizona basin for months and when the skies at last opened up, the parched and cracked desert floor shed torrents like a vinyl floor. Jerod drove slowly. He was keenly aware of the many lives dependent on his arriving safely.

Of course they didn't know it yet. Even now, when he required no more proof, and he knew in his very soul the truth he had witnessed, Jerod couldn't help but think how it would appear to this young couple in Tucson's suburbs.

The streets were black with reflective light that swam before his eyes. Jerod peered through the windshield and thought he would stand a better chance looking through the bottom of a Coke bottle. He tried to make out the house numbers; thirteen-thirty-seven. He was looking on the right side of the street anyway. Two houses up was thirteen-forty-one and Jerod pulled to the curb.

Jerod ran, hunkered down under the collar of his jacket, and rang the doorbell. He wasn't left standing in the rain long. Dan opened the door and brought him into the living room.

The house was modest, one of the older homes in Tucson. Jerod stood reluctantly on the shiny hardwood floor and watched a puddle form around his feet.

"I'm sorry about this," He apologized.

"No, please, it's my fault! I put the throw rug at the back door for Slouch, the dog. Well, you know the dog?"

Dan felt awkward and wasn't sure what to do next. He reached for the small rug between the living room and the kitchen and set it in front of Jerod for him to wipe his feet. Jerod hung his jacket on the coat rack and sat down on the sofa.

"My wife Ryann is with Mandy right now. She'll be here in a little while. We can't leave her alone."

Jerod could see Dan wince with the pain of their situation. He also saw there was no hostility toward him. At least temporarily, Dan was a beaten man.

"Would you mind if I see Mandy?"

Jerod followed Dan down the hallway, and as they drew closer to the child's bedroom, he felt a cold that defied description. Quietly they entered the room, and Jerod was immediately struck with the room's contradiction. The colors of the curtains and bed were soft and pastel, the fabrics delicate and billowing, and the child, with her golden wisps of hair lay fragile and doll-like, lost among the bed's clouds. But the room itself was cold like a tomb, a bone-chilling cold that Jerod suspected could never be measured with a thermometer.

Ryann sat on the edge of the bed, and Jerod could see she had been talking to her daughter. He wasn't certain Mandy was awake, or even conscious. Slouch was the only animated one among them and his head jerked up with ears alert as they made their entrance.

The dog was happy to see him, at least. Slouch walked over to Jerod, wagging his tail. He whined softly in happy recognition, and Jerod rubbed his ears in greeting.

Ryann got up and took Jerod's hand and squeezed it in acknowledgement. This young woman that Jerod had met at the job site, who had fairly glowed from the excitement of chasing her dog, now looked drawn and tired. Small lines, which had no place on a woman her age, creased her mouth, and there was the beginning of crow's feet around her eyes. Jerod supposed that they had all paid a toll in one way or another. He had never thought about parenting -- the emotions, the worries, and the heavy responsibility that went into raising a child. And this was under normal circumstances, he told himself. The faces in front of him said more than the explanations that followed.

"You've met Dan, Jerod? Forgive us if we've lost our manners. It's been pretty rough." Ryann looked down on her child in anguish.

Mandy's face was splotched with the now familiar rash, and she was restlessly throwing her head from one side to another. Jerod went to the side of the bed and sat down where Ryann had been. As he had in another time and place, Jerod placed his hand on the child's fevered brow.

"We put a call into the doctor, but he hasn't called back. In this storm there may be lines down," Dan said.

They watched as Mandy's body fell still and peaceful. The immediate effect was startling, and the child opened her eyes slowly. Her eyes which had, just moments before, glowed red with the reflected fever, were clear and responsive.

"Golthlay?" Mandy said, unmistakably.

Jerod was vaguely aware that the child's parents were behind him offering an explanation for this strange utterance, but Jerod's mind was somewhere else. He recalled Bill's words, "You may find that the very question may be irrelevant, or you may find it is true." It struck him that it might be both true and irrelevant, but also necessary for the time being.

"Yes, I'm here, and I will stay here while you rest, Mandy."

Minutes went by while they all waited to see if she would, indeed, rest. Soon the fevered flush left Mandy's face and she drifted off into a deep sleep. They had to believe what they saw.

"I think we need to talk," Jerod turned around to face Ryann and Dan. "But, we need to stay close."

He looked in the corner of the room, farthest from the door, and saw the little red table and chairs.

"Could we go over there in the corner? Are the chairs sturdy enough?"

"Why don't I bring in a couple from the kitchen? One of us can sit on the bed," Dan said, and he went to fetch the chairs.

***

While he was gone Jerod prayed for the right words. Never had it been so important that he win someone over. He didn't dare allow himself to think the word argument. There was the danger it might become reality. No, he had to convince Ryann and Dan that their daughter had only one way out of this and that was to enlist the help of a shaman. Oh sure, he thought. And while this seed of doubt sought a furrow to bury itself in, Jerod fought his way back to his own certainty, purposely ignoring how it appeared when named.

By the time Dan returned, Jerod thought he had a handle on it. There was a still place inside which listened to more. "Something more," he thought. Dan brought the chairs, and quite naturally he and his wife allowed Jerod the place on the edge of the bed, closer to Mandy. Jerod took a deep breath and began.

"Ryann, after I left you and Slouch, I went home and did some reading about Valley Fever and other things. First of all, I believe you're right about my rash. I believe that's what I have. Probably a mild case, except for one symptom I haven't read much about -- hallucination. Books refer to delirium, which I suppose is a nicer, more acceptable, way of saying hallucination, but the symptom is underplayed and never explained. I've thought about the cause of the disease being fungal, and how the spores from other fungi and their larger group of thallophytes have been known to cause people all through history to hallucinate. The fever could cause it, I suppose. Unless you try to make sense of *what* I am hallucinating. And what Mandy is hallucinating."

Jerod paused when he saw a look of recognition on Dan's face.

"Do you mean to say you believe there is some sense to whatever Mandy is hallucinating?" Dan asked.

Ryann was about to add something, but caught herself and turned back to Jerod.

"Yes, I do," Jerod said in complete earnestness.

"Ah, come on! This is crazy." Dan protested.

"Why don't you hear me out and then you decide." Jerod managed to keep his tone level and fair. There was no place for sarcasm in his voice, he reminded himself.

"Please, go on," Ryann said.

"I'd like to," Jerod said simply. He went back to his first experience and recounted his fear and bewilderment when hearing the rock speak to him. Jerod even confessed his concern that alcohol had played a part.

"Frankly, I thought it had to be the D.T.'s. I'm a recovering alcoholic, which means I abstain because there is no cure. But delirium tremens, or the D.T.'s as they're known, is a well-known withdrawal syndrome. I've been with some guys when they're going through this, and it's not pretty. It has been part of my own recovery to help other alcoholics when they're in detoxification. They see and imagine things that terrify them.

"Anyway, I fell off the wagon, went out one night and drank heavily. When this happened I just concluded I had taken it all a step too far. It can happen like that.

"I can't say I was happy when I found out it wasn't the D.T.'s, because, you see, it didn't get better. I wasn't drinking and it got worse!"

Ryann could see the effort required for Jerod to continue. This was confession that didn't come easy and she sensed there had to be a deep motive for this man to reveal such doubts about himself.

"Before it did," Jerod continued, "I went to an AA meeting here in Tucson. I haven't been here long, and so I just picked up a referral to a meeting out on Canal Road."

Dan thought he recalled seeing the road on the way to work. The area was the home of local Apaches, and it had fascinated Dan to watch their small children playing barefoot alongside the road.

"At the meeting I met an Apache medicine man by the name of Bill Martinez. We went out for coffee after the meeting, and I told him everything I've told you up till now. We agreed to meet the next Friday, today, and I promised to bring the rocks and fossil I had dug up."

"Where are you going with this?" Dan interjected.

"Please, Dan, be patient. I think I have an idea," Ryann said.

"Things got worse after last week." And now Jerod felt the strain of relating his experience. He could hear his own voice as he spoke, and finally just allowed this form of detachment to insulate his feelings.

He told the story of his trip to the mountain, the sick child, the Native man who asked for his help until the shaman returned. Jerod tried to recreate the realness of his visit on the mountain, and the disoriented feeling of the "rushing" as he came and went. It wasn't until the end that Jerod told the Thearles the name of the man was Golthlay.

Ryann and Dan were dumbstruck.

"Golthlay. That is the name Mandy has called out, the name she called you!" Ryann's voice was a harsh whisper and its underlying urgency reached her daughter's subconscious, and Mandy began to stir. Jerod turned and placed his hand on the child's shoulder, and she immediately relaxed.

"I'm afraid it gets stranger, yet," Jerod said. "Golthlay was, is, Geronimo's Apache name."

"Oh Christ! That's enough!" Dan had listened patiently, though it had taken every bit of his will power for him to remain quiet while this man wove a tale that belonged in a Grade B movie. But, he'd be damned if he was going to allow this to continue.

"You come in here with this cockamamie story and think you can take over! Do you really believe this so-called vision of yours has anything to do with my daughter? Because, if you do, you are crazy!"

"Dan! Please! You're going to make her worse!" Ryann pleaded.

"No, Ryann. Let me answer his question. He must hear it," Jerod answered evenly. "Yes, I do believe it has everything to do with your daughter. I know it in my soul. And if you're honest with yourself, you do too."

"Bullshit!" Dan hissed, and got up and left the room.

Jerod felt iced by Dan's cold blue eyes and yet he felt no animosity toward this young father, Mandy's father. Wouldn't he say the same thing, or worse? The truth was, he could identify more with Dan than he dared. To even entertain the idea of placing your child in the hands of a charlatan ... and that was how Dan surely had to see him ... was bordering on child abuse.

He knew better, however, and for the moment he was the only one that did. Jerod rubbed his face with his open palms. It was a gesture that cleared the cobwebs from his mind and helped him focus on the task ahead, but Ryann mistook it as an act of futility and gently protested.

"You mustn't get discouraged, Jerod. You can't. There is too much at stake."

Jerod looked up and his eyes searched hers. "Are you saying you believe me?"

"I don't know," Ryann fumbled for the words. "I guess what I'm saying is it has nothing to do with whether I believe you or not. It's true. Things have been happening, even before Mandy came down with Valley Fever. Out of the blue, she'll talk about something that doesn't make sense to us. Like her shoes. She didn't want to leave them outside because she said the last time she was here she never saw them again. What did she mean, the *last time she was here*?

"Dan knows all this and he just can't deal with it. Please be patient with him. It's not easy for him to accept the fact that he can't take care of the problem, whatever it is."

"I'll be patient, Ryann," he assured her, "but he must accept this because Mandy needs help now! There is an urgency in the timing. Again, I have to tell you what I know ... and risk whether you believe it or not."

"Go ahead," Ryann said.

"Bill Martinez has helped me to understand. We are involved in some sort of parallel world; a warp in time where the events in one age run parallel to another. It's created a window of opportunity, one where we can change the fate of some people, perhaps Yellow Bird, Golthlay's people, and Mandy.

"And even ours," Jerod continued, "because we are touched by the events. This law of cause and effect reaches beyond the grave and into new life. The law, itself, evolves."

Ryann saw Jerod giving words to some of her own thoughts. In the deeper recesses of her mind she had wondered if Mandy's comments had been memories or ... Ryann shut off such speculation, because it didn't go anywhere. Both she and Dan had ended their questions with themselves, but they had posed them to each other and it was time to face up to that. A warning sounded in her head ... don't shut off the questions, just because you don't have the answers.

"You must help Dan understand Mandy's disease is just a symptom, and we must treat the cause." Jerod watched Ryann's animated face, as each step in logic crossed her countenance. He headed her off before she asked his famous question.

"You want to know how, right? Well, the medicine man is coming. Bill Martinez is coming."

***

Chapter 16

THE PILGRIMAGE

THE PILGRIMAGE

The first light of morning was quickening and the sky's deep blue faded, as did the brilliance of the stars. The holy man had been on his mule for some time, and his joints and muscles ached. It was not just the trail ride, but the effort of concentration in the dark. With morning came the first stirring of air, and the breezes lifted from the canyon below and sailed in upward patterns, rising against the mountainside. The cool air flowed over the old man's bare legs, sweetly restoring a sense of more youthful days.

Years had marched on, and each year it became more difficult to keep pace. Dee-O-Det asked Usen, in the manner of his frequent way of conversing with Him, if He intended to give him a few more good years. Or would He relinquish him to the blanket, where he could live out his days sitting in the sun telling the younger children tales of The People? Just as the evening's sleep was welcome to one who gave great effort during the day, the old man thought the blanket more enticing with each passing winter. But, he would not make it so by willing it. He knew the stubbornness required to live and fought the luring comfort of the long sleep.

After all, it was Dee-O-Det who understood the meaning of sacred ground. In their many conversations at Golthlay's fire, the two men, chief and holy man, would talk on into the night. He had shared his wisdom, which had come in good part from his careful adherence to the Way of Life, and Golthlay had listened. Golthlay had been a good student and Dee-O-Det thought if it hadn't been for his inability to grasp the meaning of sacred ground, and that of his terrible temper, he would probably be a holy man, too. The old man reminded himself of the foolishness of his words. If one is ready to travel the Path, then he is on it. There is no place for allowances or exceptions.

But the holy man knew that each man creates his own reality, each one as limited or as advanced as he may be. From experience we determine possibility. From opportunity we create. It was Golthlay who had the gift of dreams and visions, but he struggled with his own acceptance of what he saw. And it was Dee-O-Det who accepted truth, but now in his old age had found his power waning as his spirit was drawn beyond.

The child had changed all that and so had Golthlay's dream. The holy man's attention, and Golthlay's, was brought back to this world with complete purpose and focus. The task before them was their sacred ground. It would be so. They would seek the power, each in his way.

The path was becoming more difficult. Rock slides had obliterated the trail in places, and the uncertain ground became a treacherous maze of choices. The mule, slow and calm, picked carefully the next placement of each hoof. The mule would not be panicked by the unknown ahead, the confusion of his present choices, or the anxiety of his rider.

"Usen, grant me the wisdom of my four-legged brother," the old man called out, lifting his eyes in search of the same two rocks to which Yellow Bird had pointed.

***

The morning grew older, and the breezes, which had earlier caressed the old man's body and even his soul, became more frequent and grew stronger. Sudden gusts of wind blew whistling along the ledges and through the pines left barren and bent through long endurance.

It was only hardy life that survived here in the home of the Mountain People. The pines that clung fiercely, and even the giant rocks that Dee-O-Det knew were sentient, stood guard as he passed along the trail once traveled by his ancestors.

One of the old man's feeble hands searched his belt, passing over his knife, and clutched his familiar medicine bundle. He brought with him his power, as great or as small as it might be, and knew even while he sought its comfort that it had never been as formidable as he hoped it to be.

Under his hand he imagined the contents of the leather pouch; contents kept hidden from the eyes of others, and medicine seldom called on by the holy man. The hoddentin was most frequently used, and he squeezed two gnarled fingers through the opening of the pouch and pinched a generous amount of pollen from the inner bag. Dee-O-Det flung the yellow dust into the wind and it was carried before him as a wind-borne gift to the Medicine People.

He did not pry further in the bag. This was not yet the time, but he envisioned the other objects, phylacteries of special power. There was the small war club fashioned from the purifying sage, and a small amount of the herb istafiete, and he lifted the bag to smell its heady fragrance. Deeper inside, wrapped in a piece of buckskin, he knew would be his moon stone. This small stone, which came to him from far away, carried the power of sight when placed underneath his tongue. And there was the green stone, duklij, a piece of malachite which was used to bring rain during times of drought, and would also make a weapon shoot accurately when a small piece of this stone was tied to a gun or arrow. There were the four eagle-down feathers and lastly the Black Wind, a lightning-riven pine twig, shaped as a small cross.

The holy man did not now distinguish between the powers wrapped carefully within his bag, but knew the summation to be his medicine; a medicine grown old, and unchallenged, and perhaps in need of rejuvenation. If he was worthy, the Medicine People would identify and name his power, his sacred ground.

The journey was becoming strenuous for the mule. The path grew steeper and increasingly narrow. The holy man knew the mule would only balk when he found the trail impassible. It was up to the old man to consider an alternate plan, if it were necessary to abandon the beast. The way ahead was seldom visible for more than ten yards, as the path wound, crossing back and forth on the mountain. There was seldom a level place to leave the mule, or one secure enough for either man or beast. The wind was wicked now, and he found the trail slower, and the mule increasingly reluctant to set one foot ahead of the other.

As he came around one bend he saw a shallow gully; a glen protected by heavy brush. This he thought to be his last opportunity to leave the mule. The animal would be safe enough here, as long as there were no mountain lions hunting nearby. Dee-O-Det unburdened the pack animal and tethered him to the strongest pine, still within reach of tall grasses for browse. There, beside his mule the old man ate a meal of venison jerky and ashcakes. He took his remaining cache of food and pulled it high into the tree with a rope.

Uncustomary as it was to show affection to an animal that might very well be eaten during a time of hunger, the holy man put an arm around the beast in a moment of silent commune. Then gathering his blanket, bow, arrows, and lance he took up the trail on foot. He rounded the next bend and saw his decision had been a good one to leave the mule behind. Here only a man could pass. Using his lance as leverage and balance, he sought a foothold where none was offered.

The trail widened again, but became steeper. Clouds flew in over the mountain, and he suspected the wind was bringing in a storm. A storm in this area could be swift and life threatening to those who weren't prepared. The danger to any poor souls caught at the bottom of the canyon would be fatal, as the water would rush swiftly through the narrow gorge taking everything in its path.

This was not Dee-O-Det's concern. His was the wind that now tore at his clothing, battling his progress up the side of the mountain. The wind was erratic, and if he was not vigilant he knew a sudden gust would sling him from his precarious position and over the edge. He labored with the wind at his back, all the while preparing for the moment when it would circle around and cause him to lose his footing.

The sky had turned dark quickly, in the way only those who have lived in narrow valleys could know. Lightning flashed in short bursts of light, soundless in the distance, but moving forward. He had walked all afternoon and knew the peak was close. He could feel the spirits of the Mountain People, and he made his mind receptive. In the growing roar of wind he sought a calm spirit.

As he climbed over the rise, the path now strewn with boulders, an animal stench reached his nostrils. Dee-O-Det knew the smell. It was bear; a rank and overpowering stink that blanketed the area, successfully warning wary intruders of the bear's territory.

The holy man committed. The cave of the Mountain People lay ahead and behind, already conquered, was the point of indecision. The old man gripped his lance and stepped silently on the rocks between two large boulders. He knew this might very well be his last hunt and found the thought tolerable, even beckoning. He was old and weary.

And yet he was not ready to give up this life. In his breast still beat the drum that accompanied his mission and he felt the renewed passion of a holy man's quest. Nothing could come between him and his source of power, except Life Giver.

As he renewed his pledge, there before him rose a huge and towering creature, a Grizzly. The bear's giant jaws gaped open emitting a horrendous roar. Dee-O-Det could see each terrible tooth, and knew the distance between him and the creature would not allow for time or strategy. The wind had worked against him here as well, blowing generally upward and carrying his scent.

The holy man's focus was keen and he opened his soul, allowing Usen to light the way. He crouched, still holding fast the lance and moved in closer. The giant Grizzly was made angrier by this open challenge and roared with rage.

The bear came at him with surprising speed, his confidence bolstered by the sight of his puny prey. The old man coiled his body, preparing what resistance he could for the strike that was to come. The bear lunged forward with every intention of mauling his prey on all four feet, and in that instant Dee-O-Det thrust the lance upward with all his might. Then it was too late to know whether the lance had found its mark. Dee-O-Det was thrown back against the rocks while a thousand pounds of fur hurled on him. And then he knew no more.

***

Night fell swiftly, covering the mountain top with yet another blanket of doom. The storm had broken and the clouds slung down a great wall of rain. The darkness was complete until the lightning struck. On the exposed mountain top the sky sang with electrical current, brighter than the day. Instantly on its heels was an enormous crack of thunder. The sound was everything, an earth-shattering, fearful noise that demanded undivided attention.

The old man opened his eyes. His first sensation was that of being swallowed by the earth. He felt the very womb of Mother Earth around him and was even comforted by her closeness, but then a rank stench overwhelmed him and he thought he would suffocate if he did not breathe fresh air. His arms flailed helplessly beside him. He was pinned within his mother, an unborn child seeking delivery into the world.

Then he remembered the Grizzly. Had he killed the bear, or had the bear killed him? It was still not clear who was the victor. This world, or the next, he had to breathe before his lungs burst. He struggled to find his way out from under the animal.

He fought the mammoth burden, repulsed now by the breath-choking scent of beast and blood. The ground around him turned wet and slippery. Rather than fight the tremendous weight, Dee-O-Det squirmed horizontally until he found an opening where he gasped the clean night air. He heaved one last effort against the animal's bulk and was finally free. Rain pelted his face, welcomed, nonetheless.

"Have I killed the bear?" The holy man was puzzled and still dizzy from the blow. In the eerie light that flashed repeatedly across the landscape, he saw the animal, large and still. In the rain, blue steam was rising from the bear's warm carcass, a last reminder of its life.

Dee-O-Det felt sudden regret. This large and powerful animal, who walked upright, might very well be an ancestor, or maybe one of the sacred Medicine People! He was horrified by his actions, and laboring to his knees he began to pray to the spirit of all bears. It was Grandfather Bear he had offended.

"Oh, Grandfather Bear forgive me! I came to ask for the return of my healing power, and instead I am afraid I have angered you. I have climbed this miserable mountain to beseech you to fulfill the purpose of the life of this old man!"

A bolt of lightning streaked down from the sky, striking the cave's entrance in an explosion of thunder and sparks. The old man tried to grasp the earth, clawing frantically at the rocks beneath him as the ground shook. He was certain the earth was in its death throes and he would be thrown loose and cast off as a rider on a dying horse.

The earth rumbled as the storm, that was now directly above, released its fury on the exposed peak of the mountain. The air hummed with electricity as positive ions flowed up from the earth. The old man hovered close to the ground and received his answer from the Medicine People as they spoke to him through Grandfather Bear. The bear's power was mighty and he prayed he would be found worthy.

He watched as the storm passed overhead, leaving the sky suddenly clear. The wind died, the earth lay quiet, and Dee-O-Det rose to his feet, his eyes all the while on the mouth of the cave. He felt refreshed and virile and understood this to be part of an answer, and now he knew he must explore the cave. He walked easily to the portal of the cave and was amazed at the absence of arthritic pains that had plagued his joints.

Once inside the holy man saw the walls of the cave recede in an increasing arch. There, on the stone floor a few steps directly in front of him, the lightning had struck and made a fresh break in the rock. A shallow hole revealed a rock of unusual shape, and he picked it up to take a closer look. He took it to the entrance where the stars now shone, bathing the mountaintop in a friendlier light. The holy man recognized the stone as that of a fossilized bear bone. He knew it to be a rare revelation of another time -- the time of the Mountain People, he thought. This was a sacred bone of Grandfather Bear!

Shameless tears fell from the old man's eyes. He had been chosen to receive the strength and power of bear. And not just any bear. As great in size as was Grizzly, other bears once roamed the world, and of those Grandfather Bear had been the largest.

Would his quest end here? Certainly, his prayers were answered and he was empowered to help the girl child and the others of his people who were sick. And yet he stood, looking in the cave, feeling somehow there was more.

As his eyes adjusted to the darker interior, he noticed how the starlight illuminated an inside wall. There a drawing, primitive and obscure, caught his attention. The talking pictures began with many of The People, fat and productive, shown hunting and gathering, and going about other daily tasks. It was a successful life, clearly depicting a happier time.

The second scene painted times as they were now, and the shaman saw the drawing was more recently done. But even the vivid colors showed a more dismal plight. The People, fewer in number, lay sick and weakened.

The huge wall was easily divided into three equal sections, with the two pictures occupying two-thirds of its surface. Conspicuously, the blank third stared back at the old man.

And then he remembered Golthlay's dream and the cave's talking pictures Yellow Bird had shown him. He was certain, when Golthlay had conveyed the dream, The People's destiny was revealed. It had been a communication of things to come, or of the possibility of things to come. But it was not fixed in stone. The future was not recorded here anymore than it existed in the present.

He tried to remember the third picture, to see Golthlay's vision. The shaman went out into the clear night to search for a stone that would be a suitable tool. He found several pieces of granite and returned to the wall. He began to work, recalling Golthlay's words:

"Here was a great wikiup of the White Man. Children, both White and Apache, were playing in front. They seemed happy enough and well fed. As I drew closer to the painting, I saw that Yellow Bird stood in the doorway of the wikiup and in her hand was a book of talking pictures."

The light of day began to fill the cave entrance, and the holy man was still at work. He regretted not having the paints of his people. Thinking this over, he decided that it was right for others to give color to the vision, just as others would live to see the vision become reality. His part was solely to seize the opportunity provided by Golthlay's communication, and to record it as sacred ground.

The holy man laid out his blanket, making his bed in front of the wall of the cave. He had worked hard, laboring with the primitive carving tools. Although he was weary, he was satisfied. He knew that he had faithfully recorded the third picture. He fell asleep immediately and woke later to the sound of a raucous blue jay.

The sun was directly overhead and the holy man hurriedly prepared to get under way. The journey home would be easier, if the clouds didn't decide to double back. Right now the trees and rocks sparkled with reflected light, the wind had died and there was little to recall the night's drama -- except for the Grizzly. The giant bear's carcass lay in its own pool of blood, the lance protruding from its breast and broken where the animal had hit the ground.

The old man was undecided what to do. There was no way he could pack the animal down the mountain. Even two men and a mule would have a difficult time. To not take the animal was wasteful and a dishonor. His people could use the bear grease to oil their guns and the women would use it on their hair. The meat would be eaten and the skin would provide warmth when winter came. Reluctantly, he decided to send a hunting party when he returned. They would have to take their chance against the other mountain predators, and the Mountain People would decide the outcome. Before he left the mountain, he did cut off the bear's savage claws. They would help cure his rheumatism, he thought.

***

The mule was patiently waiting for him when the old man descended. The pack animal brayed his welcome, and Dee-O-Det generously showed his affection by slapping and cuffing his old friend. He saw the animal had fared well, drinking from a pool of water left behind from the storm. He decided it was time he did the same and ate the remaining food from his cache. Carefully securing the new additions in his medicine bundle, he refastened the leather pouch to his belt, retied the blanket on the mule, and led him back on to the trail.

Two golden eagles soared through the canyon, circling and searching for fresh prey. The rains had left and the rodents, formerly burrowed in the ground, were up and scurrying. The birds made invisible spirals, flying silently, ever seeking. Seldom did they drop a wing. The holy man regarded them from his equal vantage point as he rode seated on his beast of burden.

He listened to the high piping call of the eagles, and marveled at their strong talons and magnificent plumage, with sweeping wings bathed in gold. This was further confirmation of his own transformation, as he knew he had been visited by the messengers of the Creator.

The holy man's happiness was like light within his breast, but still he was aware of the task before him. The child, Yellow Bird, lay sick and waiting. He could feel her heart grow faint. The old man spurred the mule on to hasten the journey.

***

Chapter 17

ON ACCIDENT

ON ACCIDENT

Linda wondered if she had made a mistake. She turned the car radio dial, not sure what she was looking for, unless it was an attempt to find some comfort from the wind. Static peppered every station within range and the usual spot, which played jazz twenty-four hours a day, was gone. The incoming storm was running interference.

Maybe she was running interference. Was it just out of habit that she felt it necessary to come to Jerod's aid? Through the years of their relationship she had been drawn to this seesaw of rescue and frustration. Things had grown better, she had to admit, because Jerod had found his own balance, and her emotions hadn't been jerked into the air like a lightweight child on the high end of a teeter-totter. But here I go again, she thought. Jerod leaves a message that sounds troublesome, and I'm racing across the desert to rescue him!

On the other hand, maybe I'm the problem, she thought. She knew she had felt abandoned when Jerod had taken the job in Tucson. It was definitely a sign of Jerod's independence, but it hadn't made her feel as good as she knew it should. The truth was Jerod could function without her and though that was what she had professed to want in every argument they had, it left a vacancy. She needed to analyze this vacancy.

When she had darted out of the bank, early for a Friday, she knew she had left the impression with Pam and others that there was a personal emergency; Jerod needed her. Actually, if she confessed her fear, it would be that Jerod might not need her. The message left on the answering machine hadn't been all that disturbing. Jerod had sounded hurried and excited, but in control. Was it really she who was making their relationship stagnant by not allowing it to grow? It was something to think about.

In the meantime, here she was on southbound I-10, unable to out-race a storm coming in from the West, and she wasn't even sure why she was trying. The wind that had blustered her about, as she made her way to the car, was stronger now and in danger of whipping her Camaro into oncoming traffic. She kept her speed at fifty and decided to take her time.

Linda glanced in the rear view mirror and saw the blinking lights of an emergency vehicle. For a moment she refused to believe it was the Highway Patrol. The needle of the speedometer was hovering at fifty, and she'd even turned the lights on early as a safety measure for the weather conditions. But there was the one wail of the police car's siren, which definitely was meant for her.

She pulled over to the side and waited patiently for the officer to approach her car. The sharp looking young officer fiddled with his paper work and finally exited the squad car. Linda thought his manner just a little too casual, as he walked over to the Camaro.

"Is there something wrong, Officer?" Linda asked, struggling to keep her temper.

"Did you know you have a taillight out? Thought I'd better stop you before it gets dark and you need it," said the officer.

"No, I didn't." She felt foolishly relieved.

He asked to see her license, and suggested she stop at a gas station to have the tail light checked.

"There are several stations at the next off ramp, just a couple miles up the highway. I'll let you go with a warning this time," he added.

A bit condescending, Linda thought. The officer's face broke into a smile as he handed back her license. He waited for Linda to pull back on to the highway, and several minutes later passed her with a wave.

***

Linda figured it wasn't a wasted stop; she had less than a quarter-tank and would need to buy gas before reaching Tucson. She drove into the first service station and saw there was a car at each island. Pulling in behind an older Buick, she turned off the ignition, expecting to wait her turn at the unleaded pump.

The windows were down in the car ahead and Linda could hear the woman in the passenger seat. Her voice droned on in a high-pitched whine. The driver, an elderly man, was suffering a tirade of insults, as if he were long accustomed to being on the receiving end. Linda listened, curious and yet somehow uncomfortably embarrassed.

"I told you this is the wrong pump! Do I have to tell you everything?" the woman nagged. Catching her own contradiction, she added, "From now on, I'm just going to leave it to you. Do you hear me?"

The old man didn't protest. In fact, Linda suspected he had managed to remove his mind from this scene, just as he probably had from many others over the years. He calmly turned on the ignition and drove the car in to the line at the pump marked regular. Linda pulled up to the space the man had vacated, and waited for the attendant.

A gangly teenager, wiping his hands on a grease rag, hurried over and asked how he could help. Linda told him to fill it up and asked if he would check the taillight.

"Probably a fuse!" he said, with all the wisdom of his youth.

Later, on the road, Linda thought about the scene she had just witnessed. When did the old couple's relationship become like that, she wondered? When the woman became increasingly manipulative did the man become more dependent? Or, was it the other way around?

Maybe she needed to dominate the relationship, because he couldn't or wouldn't make decisions, Linda reasoned. But then she thought of the big question, why were they still together? She couldn't avoid the answer, it was too obvious. They chose to be together. Maybe it wasn't a conscious decision, but it wasn't an accident. They needed each other: one to be a victim, the other to be the victor.

Was that where she and Jerod were heading? The idea repulsed her for one reason more than any other. It wasn't romantic! She laughed explosively, and then laughed again at the idea of laughing alone in the car. But there was truth to it, she knew. She wouldn't be attracted to Jerod if he allowed her to control the relationship. That would be too great a price to pay.

How much better it was to celebrate ones own uniqueness and individuality, Linda thought. It probably wasn't an accident that she felt more attracted to Jerod now than ever before. He was in control. She missed him, but the vacancy she had felt was the absence of his presence, nothing more.

It had begun to rain and it quickly became a deluge. Linda made a decision. She would drive straight to Pete's. Whatever errand Jerod had gone on, he would handle it, she was certain.

***

Jack sat in the BMW until the parking lot cleared. He looked out on the asphalt swimming in oily water and thought the world a dreary place. Had it always been this way and he just hadn't bothered to notice? He couldn't remember the reason why he felt he had to get away. What had been the great urgency, anyway?

He had walked briskly through the rain to the car. The change in weather hadn't registered in his mind until he felt his wet shirt cling to the leather seat. Once inside he impatiently tore open the envelope Lester Gaines had handed him before he left the plant. It had just never occurred to him that this is what it was. These were his severance papers: a pink slip and two checks, one his regular paycheck and the other included his vacation pay, profit sharing, and two weeks severance. He stared at the total. It was hefty. But it was also final.

Jack was certain Dan had been targeted for the layoff. He had been confident of so many things just a week, a day, an hour ago. The unraveling of his life, or the way he viewed his life, was as illusive as the mirage in the rain.

Several saguaro cactuses hovered on the horizon beyond Sin Par's barbed wire-edged fence. They wavered in the rain, struggling to hold their shape. Jack felt he understood them. All of his substance was in doubt. The great sense of purpose he had felt earlier ... his adrenaline, his anger ... it was gone, dissipated like the linear form of the saguaro. He tried desperately to recapture the feeling, the rage, because somehow it meant survival. This twisted, deformed vitality was the closest thing to living Jack had known.

Under this labor he sat recounting the events which had led to this sudden impotency. He backed up and recalled the phone call to Linda Caulfield's brother. The recording replayed in his mind. Linda's boyfriend had gone to Dan Thearle's house, and she would probably meet him there. They were all in it together. They had plans to ruin him, and they would get away with it if he didn't stop them. Oh yes, he knew now. He had a mission. He had a reason.

The guard at Sin Par's gate seemed relieved to see Jack leave. He was sure the guard knew this was Jack's last day. He probably thought it was amusing that he still had his own flunky rent-a-cop job and would be at his station on Monday morning, while Jack would be pounding the pavement looking for work.

The BMW peeled rubber, leaving another oily black layer on the wet parking lot. Jack squealed out on to the highway. He was beginning to feel better. He was angry. Jack barreled down I-10, easily passing more cautious drivers. He didn't notice the driver in the blue Camaro make a last-minute decision to take the next turn off. Jack's destination was a few miles farther.

Jack could feel the BMW skim the surface of the freeway and knew he was probably hydroplaning, but it didn't bother him. In fact, it somehow increased his sense of power, of being invincible. The speedometer climbed rapidly to 60, 70, 85, 95, and then he was suddenly reading the signs indicating his turn-off up ahead.

Jack cut across the lanes of traffic, neatly maneuvering the BMW in the last possible instant to complete the exit. The off ramp was a straight shot to the traffic light at the cross street, and the car obediently responded to Jack's foot on the brakes.

Rain pummeled the car and the roar filled Jack's eardrums until he thought they would burst. He could feel the mounting pressure coarse through the artery to his neck and head. He sat, helplessly waiting for the red light to turn green, drumming his fingers on the dash. Without freedom of motion the old useless impotence began to circle the fringes of his mind, and Jack would have none of that.

The light flashed green, and the BMW lurched ahead in the rain. The tires strained to grip the road, as he swung left, slamming his foot on the gas. There were no other cars on the road. There was nothing ahead for a hundred yards until the railroad crossing.

The windshield was under water, beautifully splintering the red light pulsating on the other side. Jack's last thought was of the storm's beauty and how removed he was from it.

***

Dan paced the living room floor and felt his heart pump in anxiety. This whole mess was getting out of hand. He had left Mandy's bedroom raging, but now that he had abandoned those he cared about, as well as the problem, he felt guilty, worried, and terribly inadequate. Stomping out on Ryann and Jerod was not going to solve anything. It wouldn't change events and it wouldn't help his daughter.

This was all stuff from another world. Dan thought of himself as a pragmatic sort of guy, used to dealing with the tangible, material world. This chasm, breaching the unknown, was too wide and deep to leap across. But even so, he knew it was too late; he was in mid-flight. God help me, he thought, God help all of us.

The living-room window was illuminated by a brilliant lightning display, followed by a crack of thunder. Dan's first thought was that a huge timber was breaking above his head. It could very well be the tamarack tree. He should be accustomed to Arizona's thunderstorms by now, he reminded himself.

The light in the kitchen began to flicker and then went out altogether. Dan turned on the television to check if it might be a light bulb instead of the household current. The TV screen remained black and Dan could hear Ryann call from the hallway.

"Yeah, it must be the storm! I'll get the candles." Dan answered.

He found his way to the kitchen and the pantry cupboard. The frequent flashes of light made him think of the strobe light on a dance floor. His own movements looked jerky to him, as if he were part of an animated movie. It was a confusing illusion. All of his extremities' more smooth and fluid motions were frozen in nanosecond frames of time. For a moment there was the hint of a connecting thought. It, too, danced in and out of sight.

Dan took down the odd-sized pieces of candles and their holders. This was one shelf in the kitchen which was becoming very familiar. He reached to the back and felt for the kerosene lamp. No telling how long the lights might be out, he thought. He took the matches from the drawer below and lit the lamp. With the lamp and several candles, he returned to the living room.

The lights came back on and held, and Dan stood watching the television screen fill with the news in progress. The reporter was standing in the rain in front of an apparent accident. He held the hood to his yellow slicker in fierce determination against the whipping wind. Lights were blinking and reflecting crazily in the pools of water on the street.

"Greg, it looks as if the engineer never saw the car," the reporter was saying. "I suppose we'll never know if the driver saw or heard the crossing lights in this fierce storm. There has been one fatality, the driver of the late-model BMW. We're told the engineer and several passengers have been transported to local hospitals with minor to serious injuries. This is Don Weber, Channel 4 News, at the intersection of Franklin and State. Now back to you, Greg."

Dan knew it was Jack Owens. He knew it with a certainty he couldn't have explained if someone had asked. His legs felt weak and rubbery and he sat down on the sofa, his arms still laden with the lamp and candles. And then, as suddenly as the television had come on, it was out again, along with all the lights in the house.

Again, he felt the strobe-light effect. Except this time Dan saw it as a moment caught and removed from a natural flow of events. If it were saved somehow, he thought; if it could be transported and then transplanted into another time. To those who were witnesses it would appear out of context, unexplainable and confusing. Just as it does to me, he thought.

Dan took his primitive lighting back to Mandy's bedroom. Ryann was sitting on the braided rug with Slouch's head in her lap, calmly stroking the dog. It seemed to Dan there was an affinity between the two he had never noticed before. He set down the kerosene lamp and a lit candle on the table beside Mandy's bed, and asked Ryann if they could talk, alone, in the living room. Ryann looked up acknowledging his request, and Dan extended a hand to help her off the floor. Jerod assured them he would call if Mandy asked for either parent. Dan picked up the candle as he and Ryann left.

As was customary, they went to the kitchen where most of their conferences had taken place. The dark room with its erratic shadows, cast by the lightning splashing across the walls, wasn't the same old cheerful place. Ryann asked Dan if he wanted coffee and, when he nodded, she proceeded to put a pot on the stove.

"I've just heard some bad news, Ryann," Dan said solemnly. "There's been an accident, a train and a BMW. I believe it was Jack Owens."

Ryann looked confused. Even in the dark Dan could see she hadn't understood how he had come on this information, and until she did, her brain wouldn't let her accept it as fact.

"The television came on for just a minute. It was the news, and a reporter was at the scene."

"Oh, my God!" Ryann's hand went to her mouth and she sat down quickly. "What? How? Lisa! Lisa doesn't know. And, oh God, the children."

"I know honey, but the police have ways of tracking down relatives. When the phone lines are repaired, I'll call and let them know her destination."

Ryann began to cry softly, tragically. Dan went over and held her in silence. For several minutes he did his best to comfort her and then he spoke.

"Something just happened in the living room a little while ago and it has me thinking," he said, "But first of all, I want to apologize for walking out. I was angry, but that's no excuse."

Ryann tried to convey her understanding, but Dan interrupted her.

"No. No matter what is going on, we're here because Mandy needs us. She has to be able to believe we'll be here for her. And the same goes for us. I'm not copping out, okay? You can count on me. It just got a little heavy in there, but I think I'm all right now."

Ryann's tears and smile were muffled in Dan's shirt. "I never had any doubt," she said.

"Anyway, as I was saying," Dan continued, "the lightning was shooting sudden flashes of light, and then the electric light was blinking in much the same way. It reminded me of the strobe lights when we were in college, remember?

"Do you think time works like that? Maybe a section is just yanked out, and maybe it could show up somewhere else, in another era, for instance?" Dan didn't wait for an answer.

"Well, it occurred to me, but what still bothered me was, *why*? Then the television came on! Another example of a flash of light, or a flash of time. Except, of all the programs on TV, of all the crap, why, during that instant, was the news on? Why was there suddenly a reporter at the scene of an accident involving Jack?"

Dan was a man possessed. His mind was ahead of his speech as the answers suddenly became illuminated.

"*Nothing* comes from nothing, Ryann! There is a reason for everything! I see and work with this everyday. Why should it be any different in the long run? And by the long run, I mean through all eternity.

"For every cause there is an effect. This is a law of nature I accept as naturally as I breathe. I could not be an engineer without that understanding. You can't avoid the consequences of your actions. Everything in science involves stress and resistance and the consequences!

"Would I deny a structural failure, because I hadn't found the cause? Of course not! Until I found the reason I would work on the premise that there was one!" Dan ended his words with an explosive fist on the table.

Ryann was thinking how Dan's mind had worked from a different point, but reached the same conclusion. One from the heart and one from the head, she thought. No wonder they were so good for each other.

***

Chapter 18

PARALLEL WORLDS

There wasn't anything Ryann could add. Dan was able to extract a certain logic from the madness, and it was a good thing, necessary for him. She silently poured their coffee. The aroma and the cup's warmth were solace in the candle-lit room, and for awhile they both sat absorbed in their thoughts.

"So," Dan finally spoke, "I take it Geronimo is coming to our house."

"That's right." Ryann was certain if he laughed now or, in any way, showed signs of taking this for less than the serious matter it was, she would lose Dan's help. Right now Ryann felt an animal's instinct and fierce determination to save her daughter. As she had told Jerod, it was beyond fact. Her knowledge, if it could be called knowledge, was immediate and permitted no further scrutiny. She saw herself as a mother bear standing defiantly in front of her cub, willing to fight till death in order to save its life. She knew what had to be done and was already preparing herself for Bill Martinez's visit and, to put it mildly, culture shock.

But it was apparent Dan was equally serious and in his own way making preparations. In the glare of flickering light they watched the wind-driven rain buffet the kitchen window. The unleashed powers of nature were held at bay by just a piece of clear glass. It only emphasized their home's and their family's vulnerability, thought Ryann.

They had decided to return to Mandy and Jerod when they heard a knock on the door. Bill Martinez stood on the small porch. He was wearing a worn, creased cowboy hat, which was efficiently shedding rivulets of water, and in his arms was a large burlap bag he was doing his best to protect from the rain. He was still, unmistakably, Native.

The Thearles' asked him in to their home. Their introduction was as awkward as Dan had thought it would be.

Bill ignored the moment's stiffness and reached out warmly and grasped Dan's hand. "Please call me Bill," he said.

It suddenly struck Dan the best way was to cut the formality and second-guessing and just be honest. "Jerod is in the bedroom with my daughter, and we've obviously been expecting you."

"How do you feel about all of this?" asked Bill. There wasn't any confusion about what he was saying.

Dan was equally candid. "We're supportive. We're also shocked, worried, and frankly scared for our daughter, but we are convinced you must help us."

Bill looked at Ryann and Ryann quickly voiced her agreement. "This is new to us, that's all," she said meekly.

"I understand. I will do nothing to harm your daughter. May we sit down and talk for a few minutes?"

"Of course," Ryann said. She was conscious of her own bad manners, but thought she would be forgiven her preoccupation. Ryann took Bill's hat and jacket and hung them on the coat rack beside Jerod's. Bill held fast to the burlap sack.

"We were in the kitchen," she gestured with the candle in her hand. "Would you like some coffee?"

"I'll join you there, but no thanks to the coffee," Bill said.

"As my wife said, we know very little about what is happening and probably less about medicine men," Dan confessed, when they were seated at the table. "If I remember correctly, in the little I've read on the subject, a medicine man is paid by the family of the sick person. Isn't that right?"

An easy smile broke over Bill's stoic face. "Yes. That is true. But in Mandy's case the services have been paid -- in another time and place.

"Your daughter is in a unique situation. She is most likely innocent of any violation or disrespect of power, at least in this period, or in this life. You see, all sickness is caused by some transgression of life's powers. My job is to identify the transgression in order to restore order and help return the patient's health."

In the scattered jagged light of the candle, and the lightning that flashed outside the kitchen window, Bill's presence remained steady, his voice calm.

"I am not here to replace the physician's role," Bill said. "We have been given partial information, clues, which indicate

Mandy's clairvoyance or memories are tied to Golthlay's history. In this time and place nothing can be done, and so a doctor works under a terrible disadvantage.

"The fungus that carries Valley Fever came from another time. A curing ceremony must reach across this time to learn the cause and bring about a cure."

"How in the world can this be done?" Dan had to know. He was beyond curiosity now; he was looking for spiritual understanding.

"The disease itself has presented the means," Bill spoke slowly, anticipating the time needed for the parents of the child to recognize truth and to reach acceptance.

"The hallucinations!" cried Ryann.

"Yes," said Bill.

"With Mandy's permission, I will work within her hallucination, and because Jerod is also afflicted, I will work through his. Through hallucination we will hope to recreate reality. You must think of this hallucination as unleashed imagination, and realize it can be as fearful as it sounds. This is why I am telling you, to help prepare you. The three of us, your daughter, Jerod and I, will cross over to the world of the other three: Yellow Bird, Golthlay, and the holy man. The forces that have been violated and the forces brought to cure will be unleashed, within your child's bedroom.

"Once on the path to the parallel world, you must not interfere, regardless of your concerns or fears. The danger is that someone could be lost. Do you understand?" Bill asked gently.

Ryann, and then Dan, claimed understanding, and gave their explicit consent. For some strange reason Dan looked at the clock and then remembered it had stopped.

***

It was time. Bill gathered the burlap sack, without an explanation as to its contents, and followed Dan and Ryann to Mandy's room. They entered the bone-chillingly cold room and Mandy's parents knew they had made the right decision. The difference in temperature, once they crossed the threshold, was incomprehensible. If there was an explanation for the extreme cold, they had given up trying to find it by conventional means.

Jerod greeted them solemnly. He was obviously relieved that Bill Martinez had come.

"Mandy's fever is fluctuating radically. I'm astonished how quickly it comes and goes. One moment she is terribly hot and delirious, and then when I touch her forehead she cools immediately and is calm. Should you give her some aspirin or something?" Jerod was looking straight at Ryann, appealing to a mother's special knowledge.

"It's only been a couple of hours since she had Tylenol," Ryann said, checking her wrist watch. It was difficult for her to keep the panic out of her voice.

Bill walked over to the child's bed, and bending over, he cupped his gnarled hands gently around her face.

"You have kept the fever under control, Jerod. It will be all right."

Dan knew it was time for them to leave their daughter and reluctantly reached for the candle to light their way.

"Dan, why don't you take the kerosene lamp and leave a couple of the candles here?"

Though Bill was asking a question, Dan felt certain this was what Bill wanted and so he didn't protest.

Slouch remained in his loyal spot, without challenging Bill's entrance, and Bill said he thought it best the dog stay. He was a victim of Valley Fever too, but he was also Mandy's friend. Ryann reached down and kissed her daughter's brow, and then she and Dan quietly left the room. When the door had been softly closed, Bill told Jerod the kerosene lamp would have presented a greater threat of fire.

"Quite literally, this is a flammable situation. We don't need any more fuel.

"Well, Jerod, it looks like we're about to begin. Are you here for the duration?"

"Yes, of course," Jerod answered. He couldn't even imagine not helping the child, if there was a way he could. He just wasn't sure what his role was in providing assistance.

As if reading his mind, Bill began to explain, while he carefully removed objects from the burlap sack.

Jerod had the strangest sense of taking up residence in a Salvador Dali painting. The reality of the medicine man's paraphernalia was in sharp contrast to the dreamlike aura of Mandy's bedroom. From the awkwardly shaped bag Bill drew out two headdresses, one of them a mask with feathers protruding from the top. Jerod recognized it immediately as being the mask of the Black One. It was astonishing to see the now familiar face. The headdress attached to the other mask was much more elaborate and Bill called it a chas-a-i-wit-te.

"These are but two of the masks belonging to the Gan dancers. They have been kept by The People, in hiding, for many years. The Gan represent the Mountain People and when these masks are worn their spirits are here."

The Gan headdress was made of slats of a Spanish bayonet, just as described in the book Jerod had read. The large horizontal piece was crossed at either end with a vertical piece. In the middle were the uprights, or "horns," which indicated the Mountain Spirits' guardianship of horned game. Bill explained that the large piece of tin in the middle represented the sun, and the other designs and vertical slats depicted a rainbow, clouds, raindrops, and hail. From the horizontal supports there hung feathers from the eagle and turkey, and small pieces of wood that now brushed, one against the other, making the haunting sound of a chime.

They would not wear the masks, but by placing them against the child's body the Mountain Spirits would make known their presence. Bill told Jerod that he had spent much of the time, prior to coming, in purifying his own body through fasting and a sweat bath. This would have been desirable for Jerod to do as well, he said. However, the child's crisis required Jerod's presence.

Next, from the sack, Bill unfolded a cloth that held the purifying sage. The remaining leather pouch was Bill's medicine bundle, he explained. Jerod suspected the bear fossil was kept there also.

Bill took the plate that held one of the lit candles and placed a twig of sage in the flame. A pungent smoke wafted across the room, and he instructed Jerod to carry the plate into the four directions, East, South, West and North. Jerod waved the smoke into each direction with a motion of his hand.

Slouch was intensely alert as Jerod followed the medicine man's instructions. Bill was now placing the masks against Mandy, who was becoming increasingly restless. Mandy began to protest in a language Jerod did not recognize. They were pitiful sounds, more animal than human.

"The hallucination has begun," Bill warned.

Almost on cue the room was lit with lightning and an ear-shattering crack of thunder broke overhead. Jerod was certain a tree had fallen on the roof. The room was filled with an electrical charge that hummed in a language all of its own. There was a visitor among them and its smell was overwhelming. Slouch barked, frantic that he could not pin down the invader, the direction it was coming from, or its nature.

From behind Jerod, much too close, came a roar that equaled the thunder's volume. He turned and saw a huge bear towering above him. A cavernous jaw gaped open, exposing a set of deadly, yellowed teeth. The creature's presence under any circumstances would have been unworldly, but in this room the bear's head was bent to fit under the ceiling. His dimensions were those of a prehistoric mammal.

"He is not real, Jerod. He is not real," Bill kept repeating. And Jerod thought it curious there was not a hint of panic in his voice.

Behind the monster, and a little to each side, stood two bears, both fierce, but of a smaller size. Incongruously, the little red table and chairs stood between them. Mandy's stuffed toy bears were no longer engaged in a tea party; the chairs were empty.

Slouch was barking and, Jerod thought, foolishly antagonizing the "over-matched" predators. But apparently oblivious to his barks, the first bear turned aggressively in the direction of the other two, who were snarling and snapping at him. A fierce battle began between the three. There was no indication the bears had seen any of the humans. They didn't seem conscious of their surroundings, but were preoccupied with fighting for their lives. The noise was horrendous, the smell a suffocating putrid blanket, but most of all the sight of warring bears, within just a few feet of their presence, petrified all of them.

Jerod found his body could move and he backed closer to the bed. There he noticed Bill had removed the fossil from his bundle and was holding it out from his chest. The medicine man was chanting in low, repetitious syllables.

Just as suddenly as the bears had appeared they were gone, and the bedroom, all of its furnishings, and the three of them, as well as Slouch, were caught in swift movement, fluid and slick to begin with, and then increasingly fast. Nothing was tangible. They were "rushing," but independent of one another. Jerod felt a flash of anger. He had not been prepared, and he had no time to prepare the others, or at least Mandy.

The child was thrashing her arms, searching for something to hold. She began to scream and Jerod heard the volume of her voice modulate in warped waves. Would she be able to withstand the transition? Bill held her arms as if she would spin off into eternity if he let her go. And then they were alone, to cope individually, as best they could, and Jerod tried to think of it as the eye of a storm. He knew instinctively that this implied reality of their destination on the other side. In the meantime, this was a place where nothing existed; a walled-off emptiness, an unreal, unholy condition that was only familiar because he had been here once and had lived to remember. He clung to this knowledge as his only tool, or weapon ...

The blackness slipped into the blue-black and motionless stars of the night's sky. Before Jerod became aware of the others around him, he breathed the cool, pine-scented mountain air. He took a large breath, gulping greedily, allowing the now familiar place and time to fill his lungs and soul.

Jerod was standing at the entrance of a wikiup looking out over a ledge. The sky was deep and tranquil and the twinkling stars seemed to beckon him with their brilliance. Stubbornly, he turned back to those inside, to those who needed him now. The shaman was chanting over Yellow Bird, and the child was sleeping peacefully, her small body almost covered by the ceremonial masks. Golthlay continued to smudge the child and the wikiup with the burning sage incense. It was almost over. He could feel the healing of the rite, and knew this to be a sign that he had been called on The Path. The holy man had taught him much and would teach him more, but tonight, in this moment of eternity, Golthlay had been called to be his apprentice.

The struggle would be long, he knew. It was not within the power of Golthlay to change his self, but before him was a glimpse of possibility. Only an idea now, but it hung on the horizon and beckoned as did the morning star. One day, in some point in time, in perhaps a parallel world, Golthlay would renounce his vow of Netdahe and choose to never live for death again.

The holy man rose stiffly from the blanket and motioned to Golthlay to come outside with him and let the child be. Golthlay let the blanket fall behind them, as they crossed the threshold and entered the night. The holy man spoke softly, in the reverent tone of one whose prayers had been answered.

"You must tell The People. The Mountain Spirits have restored Yellow Bird's life, and they can expect the plague of coughing disease to leave us. In return, I have pledged the return of the child to her people. When she has regained her strength, you must take her to the White Man's settlement. We both know her future there, and how she will someday work to preserve ours."

Golthlay looked up into the heavens and felt his spirit reach beyond itself. When his thoughts turned back to earth, he willingly departed.

The churning vertigo of the "rushing" returned. Jerod thought the sense of being lost in space was the loneliest feeling he had ever known. He wondered how the others were handling it -- the shaman, the child, and the dog. He was curious, where was Slouch?

Again, there was the sudden thump, a soft collision of two worlds, or time. Jerod would never really know, not in the sense that it could be explained. Maybe some things were meant to be that way, known, as in experienced.

He was not alone and Jerod felt immediate joy from this knowledge. Bill was sitting beside Mandy and the child's eyes were open wide with interest.

"Is it over? Is the ha-lu-sa-shun over now?" she asked.

"Yes. It is over," said Bill.

Slouch's nose peeked out from under the covers on the bed. He whimpered a tentative greeting.

"Slouch, where were you? Did you hide from the ha-lu-sa-shun?" Mandy struggled to sit up, and reached out with open arms to hug her dog.

"Yes, where was he?" asked Jerod.

"I suspect he had no part on Geronimo's mountain," said Bill, smiling. "But he seems to play a big part here!"

The light beside the bed came back on and the final shadows of the past retreated. Jerod told Mandy he was sure her parents would be glad to see her, and thought he'd better tell them the good news. He opened the door and saw the shadows had left Ryann's and Dan's faces, as well. The two stood waiting obediently. In the reassuring light the bedroom, no longer unnaturally cold, once again looked friendly and inviting, and Jerod welcomed them.

Epilogue

SACRED GROUND

SACRED GROUND

He was surprised when he stepped outside and met the new world. For that was what it felt like, the rain-washed, settled ground and Mandy's swing set, cleansed and sparkling in the morning sun. The intensity of colors made Dan's eyes water. Not with glare, but with the emotional summation of discovering a day that, only last night, he had held real doubts any of them would see. It was glorious, the rich varied greens of the backyard's trees, reaching tall and unburdened into the blue sky. Dan noticed the tamarack had lost a huge branch that had fallen across the roof. That explained the crashing sounds Jerod and he had heard during the night, or at least the "this side" explanation.

The limb was lying perilously over Mandy's bedroom, its jaggedly torn, white pulp raw and protruding from the tree's main trunk and its foliage covering Mandy's window. Dan would have to take care of it today and check for roof damage. Even this couldn't daunt his spirits. He felt a survivor's keen awareness and appreciation of an averted tragedy. The daylight had not diminished the night's events. It had only enhanced them.

Dan remembered the phone call he had made to Colorado when the lights had finally come back on, and again felt the chill from learning of Jack's death. It had not been easy telling Lisa Owens about the accident, especially when his own family had lived a harrowing night cheating the Grim Reaper. He could still feel Lisa's silence on the line, and think of Tracy and Thad sleeping with no knowledge of the event that would forever change their lives. Dan wondered, how would she deal with it?

There was a responsibility that accompanied survival and he was determined to honor his. But he knew his was nothing compared to what lay ahead for Lisa, raising two children without their father. He had volunteered Lisa any assistance Ryann and he could offer from Tucson, and still felt the futility in his words of sympathy.

Dan and Ryann had their Mandy, miraculously recovered and even pleading to go outside with her dog. To assure herself of their daughter's recovery, Ryann had insisted on one more day of rest than seemed to be medically warranted. Dan thought of the two of them and Slouch sleeping peacefully in Mandy's bed, where he left them to catch up on the sleep lost in another time zone. It was all the security he needed.

***

The community church, where the AA meetings were held, was taking on a new coat of paint. Jerod recognized several of the men from last week's meeting. They had paint buckets and brushes in hand and were aggressively attacking the walls.

There was none of the somberness of last week and it was obvious this was because the men were working on a common job. A Native man called from the scaffold clinging to the side of the building, and Jerod recognized Bill Martinez.

"You're early! Or, we are behind schedule." Bill wiped his hands on a rag. He climbed down and walked over to Jerod, turning to look approvingly at the work. The frame building glistened white in the afternoon sun and actually sent out an invitation of cheerful welcome.

"Wouldn't have known it was the same church," Jerod said, "if I hadn't come while you were painting it. You should have told me. I'd like to help, especially now that the rash is gone."

"You still can, if you're serious. We've a lot more to do. You haven't seen the back side. But, I forgot, you do grading. Come and see what a mess the rain made of the parking lot."

"Actually, I do have some time on my hands right now," Jerod said. "The job is going to be held up while Pete and several archaeologists play in the dirt. I guess, they're only following my example!

"You know, Bill, you and I may want to join them. You certainly have reason enough ... I mean, besides that of the Apache's history." Jerod thought a moment and then added, "After all, it is our sacred ground."

***

BIOGRAPHY

Wendy Padilla continues her writing in Southern California on her small ranch, Pa-Gotzin-Kay (the place to go – Apache). It is here where she hosts Nakwach, a community dedicated to the Red Road and Native American ceremonies, such as the sweat lodge and medicine wheel, supporting those who are now celebrating life on a spiritual path.

Wendy and her writing partner, Donna Simko, have written the **Medicine of the White Owl** and intend at least two more in a series for those who love adventure and the colorful history of New Mexico in the 1800s.